The Gyp... ...ogy

Gold and
Silver
Water

Also in the Gypsy Girl trilogy

The Parsley Parcel

The first of Freya's adventures. Will her Romany magic be strong enough to fulfil a promise and grant Emma Hemmingway's deepest wish?

A Riot of Red Ribbon

Freya's greatest challenge yet. Briar Rose and Dibby Gran have mysteriously disappeared and Freya must use all her powers to find them.

Gold and Silver Water

by Elizabeth Arnold

Mammoth

For Cheryl, my friend and Freya's,
and for Eileen, who holds the heart
of Great-gran

First published in Great Britain in 1997
by Mammoth
This TV tie-in edition published 2001
by Mammoth, an imprint of Egmont Books UK
a division of Egmont Holding Limited
239 Kensington High Street, London W8 6SA

Text copyright © 1997 Elizabeth Arnold

Cover photographs by Nigel Dickinson copyright © 2000 Film and
General Productions Ltd

The moral right of the author has been asserted

ISBN 0 7497 4594 0

10 9 8 7 6 5 4 3 2

A CIP catalogue record for this title is available from the British
Library

Printed and bound in Great Britain by Cox & Wyman Ltd,
Reading, Berkshire

Contents

1 The Crossing 1
2 Dancing Flames 4
3 Penny 12
4 Briar Rose 22
5 Strawberry Woods 31
6 Problems 43
7 The Joining 53
8 Morning Magic 64
9 The Picnic 69
10 Uncle Norman 86
11 Mary's House 92
12 Wall Painting 111
13 Happy Shoes 123
14 Changeover Time 140
15 Riddles 149
16 An Invitation 158
17 Great-gran 161
18 Shimmering Gold 167
19 Holy Water 174

20	Sweet Roses	180
21	The Christening	186
22	Church Walk	194
23	Trinity Magic	202
24	Resolution	210
25	The Legacy	212
	A Little Gypsy History	214
	Romany Words Used	216

1 The Crossing

'I don't want to cross the line!'

'Oh, come on, Penny, it won't take a moment.'

'But, Mum! *The lights are flashing red*!'

Frances Bootle sighed and gave Penny a little shove. The lights always flashed red for ages and, when the goods train eventually passed, it seemed to take for ever. They were already ten minutes late, he would be waiting.

'It's only *just* flashing, Penny. Now get a move on!'

'You said . . .'

'Penelope, *please*! Just this once.'

Penny Bootle scowled at her mother before running as fast as she could across the wooden slats indicating the country crossing. She was surprisingly agile despite her slightly heavy frame. Safely across, she held open the exit gate for her mother and baby sister.

Frances Bootle sighed with relief. Penny could

be so stubborn at times. She hurried after her eldest daughter, dragging the push-chair full of sleeping baby and newly purchased packages behind her.

Bump bump bump went the push-chair as it was hauled across the footpath sleepers. It always amazed Penny how Katya could sleep, even when the paths were rough and she could barely breathe for piled-up parcels.

'Hurry, please, Mummy,' Penny called anxiously from her side of the line, but the sound of her voice was lost. All that could be heard was the bump bump bump of the little push-chair wheels as they bounced on and off the boarded tracks.

At first, Penny didn't see the train coming. It rounded the bend filling her ears with the sound of screeching brakes, slammed on as soon as the little family came into the driver's view. Desperate horn warnings began vibrating in her head, turning her legs to water. She saw the horror on the approaching driver's face and, in that instant, her mother and sister were lost to view in its shuddering path.

Penny covered her ears in a hopeless effort to block out the final squeals of the braking train and her own fearful screams. Her body shuddered violently as she saw her baby sister, Katya, flying through the air like a pink tissue caught in a spring wind. Frances, her mother, lay by the rails, her body still but bleeding. Further down the line, the driver scrambled from his train.

Penny stood stuck to the spot in terror. Her head, which moments before was almost shattered by exploding sound, now filled with eerie silence. It seemed like for ever before she could wake up her frozen limbs and run for help.

2 Dancing Flames

'I'll not let her have my vardo . . . it's just not proper.'

I dragged a huge log from the pile stacked under the hedge to keep them dry, and pulled it towards the fire.

'She can't have it, not even over my dead body.'

I used all my strength to pick up the huge lump of wood and hurl it into the centre of the slowly ebbing flames. I love my great-gran, but she can sound pig-head stubborn at times.

Burning the vardo, well, it would almost be over her dead body; that's what it was all about. We Romanies like to die in the open. Under a wagon is the very best place. There it is warm and dry, and a Romany can feel at one with nature, in touch with the earth.

In the old days, it was always the same. Even if you were church-box-buried, all your things were

4

flamed where they stood. I kicked the fresh log with my toe, to make sure it was properly settled.

'What point is there in burning the vardo?' my mam was saying. 'It's worth a small fortune to a gorgio, and all the world to Chime.'

'Freya may be a Chime Child, but I need the vardo to cross over.' My great-gran's voice sounded petulant. 'If she wants a vardo so much, then she can build her own!'

'And are you able to turn chicken feathers into gold?' my mam retorted, her voice rising travel-miles high as it always did when she was truly miffle-minded.

I paid little mind to their squabbling, I was watching the grateful flames spring into life round the sweet-smelling pine. It was nothing new, all this arguing. It was safe like a comfort blanket. I'd heard it on and off for as long as I was remember-ing-able.

'She's a special one, that great-grandchild of yours. A Chime Child is not often born.'

'I know that! I, of all people, know that. Haven't I learned her everything? Haven't I spent every pre-cious hour, filling her head with wise-ways wisdom?'

'Chosen she is,' Mam's voice was pleading now,

'surely that makes things different? Surely that entitles her?'

I glanced round, more out of habit than anything else. My mam was cutting up carrots, and throwing them into the great iron sastra pot that we used when Kokko George, or Vashti, my married brother, came visiting. Vashti wasn't here now, or Kokko George, but Mam wasn't thinking fine-head clear. She was too busy trying to nag modern mind-thinks into my great-gran.

Great-gran sat unrepentant on the wooden steps of her vardo. A vardo is a proper Romany wagon. Our great-gran's has hand-made carvings, and a soft feather bed made as it should be, with chavi-picked feathers.

I sighed. All this yelling and pleading would change nothing. Great-gran was too locked up in the old times. If she thought that she needed the vardo to pass to the better world, then that was how it would be. We would burn her things and not cry. We would send her off with our best dancing and our loudest music. We would do it exactly as she wished. The family would obey because, even if she was ostrich-head stubborn, we still loved her.

'So much that has passed will be burned,' my

mam said sadly, hoping the soft approach might work where yelling hadn't.

'The past is locked in the head, not in *things*,' Great-gran retorted, her face real lemon-suck sour. 'The Chime Child knows that!'

I did know that, but it didn't stop me wishing I could have the vardo. It was proper old, and historic valuable. I felt as if it was already part of me. I sensed the magic carved into its ancient timbers, magic so strong that it had captured my heart when I was still all toddle-tongued. My great-gran had held me up to touch the shiny wood, letting its power flow deep into my bones.

'Bori bori,' I had said, and I remember Great-gran laughing proudly.

'Yes, Chime, bori bori, big friend.'

Despite my yearning to own that bright and happy wagon, I had no interest in their bickering. They could argue for days and days if they had a mind to. When I was knee-high I used to think my mam could change things, and that, one day, the vardo would be mine. A special wagon to help do special magic. Now I am best-part grown, and I know better. Great-gran may look old and frail, but she still rules us with a rod of iron.

The lovely sunshine vardo will end its days as

stone-cold ashes, and we will join the endless tribes with all cold metal caravans. My mam doesn't care for herself. She likes her large caravan, modern oven, and nice inside toilet, but she knows how much I love the vardo, and so she tries nag-times often to save it for me.

I chucked a smaller log into the flames, and watched them dance with joy. This time, little red and yellow feather tongues reached up to lick the sweet hazel. I watched them grow in strength until they sprouted taller than the blackening log and showed me their full-flame faces.

I stood rigid-still. The fire was talking. There in the warm curls I saw the face of Aunt Emma. Aunt Emma and I have been all-time linked by a special parsley magic, ever since Kokko George persuaded Great-gran to issue a drúkkerébema, which means a prophecy that must be fulfilled.

Aunt Emma and Uncle Jack had had to look after me then, and they are so cup-full kind that I think of them now as my gorgio family. Through the dancing flames I could see Aunt Emma clutching her new baby. I am not a baby-batty girl, but this bubbo is like a sister to me.

Something was very wrong. Aunt Emma and

Uncle Jack wore frown-worry faces, and they were calling me.

'Freya! Freya, we need you, please come!'

I crouched down, in order to see more clearly the dancing faces in the ring of fire.

'Freya, we *need* you.'

Green flames on the edge of the face flames grew taller. They flickered wildly.

'Freya, Chime Child. Go to the gorgios,' the emerald flames commanded as they grew higher and higher, nodding and bowing to stress the importance of their telling tongues.

I felt shivery scared. What if the baby was sick? I had never seen her but I felt responsible. It was, after all, my magic that had made her.

I performed the secret signs that my great-gran had so carefully taught me, and threw a wishing-stone deep into the talking flames.

'I wish to help. I acknowledge my calling. I come to help, for that is my being.'

Aunt Emma and Uncle Jack smiled at me through the orange fire-licks. Their confident smiles told me that they knew I would come. I could clearly see the baby, she seemed to be sleeping gently, so it wasn't *her* waking the dark dragons of fear in the flaring fire.

Aunt Emma pointed, so I followed her fingers. There, deep in the blue-hotness flames, I could see two more faces. One, all cheeky freckle-speckled, belonged to Mary, my gorgio friend. The other face was sullen and scared. Dark-despair eyes gazed at me from the depths of the blue-hearted fire. I felt shiver-cold despite the warming flames. I understood instantly that those eyes were the reason for my calling.

I turned to tell my mam of the magic, but there was no need.

'What did you see?'

'People . . . Gorgios.'

'What did they want?'

'Me.'

My mam and great-gran stared at me, their grumbling quite forgotten.

'I saw Aunt Emma and Uncle Jack, and most of all I saw a gorgio girl who Aunt Emma said needed me. I saw her locked-heart scared and deep-pit sad. I felt black pain and white anger. I overflowed with emptiness. I felt alone.'

For a while there was silence, then my great-gran just nodded, and my mam went back to stirring her great iron sastra pot. She threw in wild thyme and fresh coriander. She mixed them in as if her very life depended on it.

'You better eat well,' she said at last. 'Chime Child, if you are called, then you must go. Tomorrow, when the sun is freshly risen, we will take you. You have no choice but to follow your destiny.'

3 Penny

'I suppose you've brought the magpie?'

I nodded. Maggie-Magpie was in my carry bag. It hadn't occurred to me to leave her behind.

'Ah well!' Aunt Emma said, as she reached out to grab me and smother me with kisses. 'I suppose I shall have to put up with you both.'

I tried not to struggle too hard. I am a Romany and we don't need sloppy-slurp kisses to show that our hearts are pleased. I rescued my carry bag containing my kackaratchi friend, Maggie. Aunt Emma was hugging us far too hard, we were in danger of being squelched.

Once the kackaratchi was safe, I offered my face to be kissed by Uncle Jack, who couldn't wait to tell me how much I had grown. Did he really think I didn't know? My great-gran nags me half to death. 'That dress has become far too short, Freya! Sit with your knees closed, you are nearly a lady now.' Even a little Romany can't stay small-child wild for ever.

'Where's the baby?' I asked as soon as I had escaped from their clutches.

'Sleeping soundly,' Aunt Emma said, giving me a warning glance and raising her pointy finger up to her lips. 'She's lovely, Freya, I desperately wanted her to greet you but . . .' She turned her head uneasily towards the house. 'There's a problem.'

I nodded. I knew. Dancing flames filled my mind, flaring flames that licked possessively round a girl with terror-filled eyes.

'I'll show her to you as soon as I can,' Aunt Emma said. 'I can't wait. She's such a poppet, Freya, even *you* will have to be impressed.'

I was sure she was right. After all, this baby was special. I had shared her beginning.

'Why am I called?' I asked, my head stuffed full of dancing flames.

'Come and have some chocolate cake,' Aunt Emma said, looking all eye-wary again. 'It's the recipe you really like but, first, give me another hug. Freya, you seem so grown up, it's really lovely to have you here again. We've missed you so much, you know.'

'Yes, I know all that!' I said impatiently. 'But why am I called?'

This time it was Uncle Jack who made a

shushing gesture with his fingers. The sort he made when I wanted to tell him about my day, and he wanted to watch the news. I buttoned my mouth. I set it in a thin line, so they knew they had to say *something*.

'She's in there,' he whispered, and I knew that he meant the girl with the dark frightened eyes and sadness-sewn mouth.

'Now come and have that cake,' Aunt Emma said over-loud cheerfully, before dropping her voice even quieter than Uncle Jack's and adding, 'and then we'll tell you all about her.'

I listened in silence. Uncle Jack was impressed with the seriousness of my listening. Only when they left spaces did I ask questions.

'When she was four, her dad just walked out?'

'Penny was devastated. She'd always been such a daddy's girl.'

'How long was her mother, Frances, ill and depressed for? Why didn't you ask me for herbs?'

'Oh, Freya, that was ages before we met. Penny was such a help to her then, they grew so close. That's why Frances is so upset that she won't visit her now.'

'She saw her mam being train-smashed broken?'

Aunt Emma and Uncle Jack nodded.

14

'And she won't visit the hospital, not even for a minute?'

'No, darling, if we even *offer* to take her, she screams.'

I found it hard to understand. I couldn't be away from my mam, especially if she was poorly bad and needing me. I struggled to see into the mind of this strange child who hated her mother. This terrible Penelope girl, who was the reason for my calling.

'It's understandable, Freya,' Uncle Jack told me quietly. 'After all, Penny didn't want to cross the railway line, not when the warning light was red. She warned Frances that it wasn't safe to cross.'

'It was an accident,' Aunt Emma repeated, 'a dreadful accident. All of us take risks some time, all of us make mistakes.'

'It was a mistake that killed baby Katya,' Uncle Jack said grimly. 'It was a very foolish risk to take, crossing the line with a child and a baby, especially when the light was red.'

'It was an accident!' Aunt Emma repeated. 'She's been punished enough with her legs all smashed and baby Katya being killed. Frances is sick and riddled with guilt. She needs forgiveness, not anger. She needs to know that her daughter loves her.'

'But she doesn't!' Uncle Jack told Aunt Emma for what must have been the hundredth time. 'At this moment she doesn't, and that is understandable too.'

I nodded. While they had been telling me, I had felt as if I was on a seesaw of love and hate, locked tangle-tight.

After a while, Penny Bootle allowed herself to be led into the kitchen. She was settled into her chair as if she was three and not nearly eleven. Aunt Emma is ever so kind, she's fostered loads of difficult children, including me.

'Hello, Penny,' I said, offering her my sunniest smile.

Penny ignored me. She sat staring straight ahead, as if I had kept my mouth buttoned up all tight.

'Have some chocolate cake, Penny.' Uncle Jack pushed the plate towards the mousy-haired girl with the dark staring eyes. 'Aunt Emma made it extra gooey, to celebrate Freya's return.'

Still Penny Bootle said nothing. Uncle Jack cut off a slice, put it on her plate, and shoved it in front of her stubby little nose.

Penny neither looked nor smiled. If I had behaved like that, my mam would have smacked me wicked for being so rude. I knew she was sick-head suffering, so I tried to think of her kindly, but it was thump-heartbeat difficult to do.

'My name's Freya. Aunt Emma thought that you and I could be friends. I think that could be nice . . . don't you?'

I didn't really think it would be nice at all. It couldn't be, not if even Aunt Emma needed help, but I minded my manners to please her and Uncle Jack, and anyway I had no choice. The dancing flames had commanded me.

Petulant Penny said nothing. She ate her cake as if it was rock-stale bread, and not yummy chocolate with nuts and cherries.

She drank her tea not seeming to care that it was steamy hot, and likely to burn her stuck-fast tongue.

I waited politely. Penny never even looked at me, and she certainly never smiled. Even Maggie talked to me better than that. We all waited, hoping she would say something, but she didn't. The silence swelled up, making us feel hot-sticky uncomfortable. I'm a rattle pot. My great-gran says silence is unnatural to me, so after a while my tongue shot free.

'Cat got your tongue?' I asked, my tone just a bit too sweet to be pleasant.

Po-faced Bootle said nothing. Aunt Emma and Uncle Jack pretended to be busy chewing cake. Can't speak with our mouths full, can we, Freya? So it's all up to you . . .

I tried pretending I was even more cross than I felt. I can never stop my tongue when I am shiver-spine angry. Romanies are like that, hot cross fire-mouths. It was possible that Pouty Penny was the same.

'Why is your mouth so buttoned? Can't you act normal? Can't you even get tingle-tongue mad? Can't you even say, *Freya, shut your silly gob and go home*?'

Nothing, not even a scowl, rewarded my efforts.

We all gave up. It was Uncle Jack who broke the next silence. 'It's shock,' he reminded me gently. 'The doctors say Penny is traumatised. That means seeing the accident made her so upset that she's shut herself out of our world.'

Penny Bootle sat like a great big pudding, there was no living look in her eyes. I've seen clothes-peg dolls with more life in them than her.

'Can she hear?' I asked, wondering if I had mis-understood before.

'Yes.'

'Can she see as clearly as me?'

'Yes.'

'Can she speak if she wants to?'

'Well, she can certainly scream! You only have to mention visiting her mother and she goes loopy, and poor Frances is so desperate to see her.'

I brushed the crumbs from my mouth and finished my tea. 'And this is why I'm called?' I asked, thinking how heart-stopping horrid it was going to be, trapped in Aunt Emma and Uncle Jack's posh house, with this pouty-faced girl.

'Please, Freya . . .'

'You have to help her.'

'Well, I think she's being selfish!' I turned to Penny. '*I think you're being a big selfish pudding*! You should be with your mam, helping her to get better.'

Penny Bootle didn't react at all. She continued to sit, looking wet-Sunday dull.

I found her mind-thinks very hard to understand. When my mam lost our baby, Pansy, life had still carried on. Wood was still fetched, herbs were still gathered and carefully dried, freshly washed clothes were hung out on the hedges, so they smelled summer-sweet. My mam said that, even if you're full up heart-sad, you still have to plod life's pathway. It's just that, for a while, you don't notice the view. We had shared all our tear-days, even though

19

we had not said much, for that is our way. Frances Bootle should not have to lie all alone in her hospital bed.

'At least my mam had my brothers and me, when Pansy was took.'

'Yes,' Aunt Emma agreed sadly.

'There's no escaping *my* mother,' I told Penny. 'I could try running to anywhere in the whole wide world. It would just be the same. My mam would mind-think her way back to me. Mostly, I like it like that.'

'I can understand how Penny feels,' Uncle Jack said, pushing his teacup away. 'She was so excited about her baby sister. She was even getting used to her mother having a boyfriend, and now, well, now all of that is spoiled.'

'Frances was in love, and late meeting her boyfriend. Just for a moment she let her heart rule her head. Surely you can understand that, Freya?'

I shook my head. 'I hate boys.'

'Even Tashar?'

'Well, no, but he's my best brother, he doesn't count.'

Aunt Emma laughed. 'You have taken other risks. I remember when you chanced slipping off a riverbank, and were nearly torn to shreds by thorn bushes. I recall that, on top of all that, you were scratched by a cat, and just for the sake of a half-dead magpie.'

'It lived!'

'That's not the point! The issue is, that you didn't think. You took risks and scared me half to death. If you had drowned, or been poisoned by spines, how would you have worked your magic then? Frances took a risk too, but it went badly wrong.'

I thought of not having Maggie, or Aunt Emma not having the parsley baby. That was the thing with taking a risk. You could end up with the golden egg, or a million shattered dreams.

4 Briar Rose

The baby's room was flowery-flouncy, just as I had
expected. There was everything a baby might wish
for and more. Aunt Emma saw me looking round.
'Well, we waited a long time, didn't we?' she said.
'So I spoil her a little.'

'Just as well you didn't have to wait any longer,'
I replied, wearing my teasing voice. 'The baby
would never fit into the room.'

I made my way round the mobiles and teddies
and peeked into the cot.

'She's not really a baby, is she?'

'Of course she is! Six and a half months old is still
a baby.'

I shrugged. 'She looks like you, Uncle Jack, but
her nose is yours, Aunt Emma.' I was all outside
calm, I wasn't going to let them know I was heart-
happy pleased. How could I? I am a pure-bred
Romany, not a soft-soap gorgio. 'As bubbos go she
seems OK.'

'I was rather hoping that she wouldn't have my nose,' Aunt Emma said, gently stroking the soft-skinned infant. 'It's horrid.'

'It's not!' I said, taking Aunt Emma's hand. 'I wasn't being rude. It's long and straight and regal. It's an important nose.'

Uncle Jack chuckled. 'Well, if it's like her mother's, she'll be able to smell trouble from a very long distance.'

'Not a bad gift then,' I said. 'Is she named?'

'We took a long time choosing her name. We thought about Parsley ... after your wretched seeds, but what sort of name is Parsley for such a pretty girl?'

'Quite awful,' I agreed, smothering a grin.

'So, after a lot of thinking, we chose Rose,' Uncle Jack said in a proud tone that told me I was supposed to be truly impressed.

'Why Rose?'

'We thought there should be qualities in her name that are associated with you,' Aunt Emma joined in. 'Not, of course, that it would ever be possible to block *you* from our minds.'

'So,' Uncle Jack said, 'we thought of several reasons to call our baby Rose.'

I pretended not to be too bothered with reasons

but Aunt Emma and Uncle Jack could tell I was bubble-bursting with curiousness.

'It's a flower, and we thought of your lost sister, Pansy.'

'It's aromatic, and you love herbs and flowers.'

'Roses are useful, like your parsley.'

'And, of course, they're beautiful.'

'OK, I like the name Rose. I have to, don't I, after all that? But . . .'

Aunt Emma's face paled. She had so wanted me to be pleased. I couldn't tickle-tease her any more.

'I like the name Rose, really I do, but she has to be a wild rose. They smell real nature-scented, not muddle-messed by man.' I grinned at them both. 'I'm going to give her a wagon name. After all, she is like a little bit of me. She's not a total gorgio, she can't be, not if I helped make her.'

'A wagon name?'

'You can't have forgotten, Aunt Em! Is that what having babies does – addle your brain to nothing?'

'Well, I think it does for a while,' Aunt Emma said, struggling to reach her deep-down mind. Uncle Jack and I didn't help, not a bit. We shared a nod, and a wink, and waited.

'Your proper name is Freya Boswell,' Aunt

Emma said at last. 'Your wagon name is Chime. It's like a nickname.'

I clapped my hands in delight, happy that she had remembered. Uncle Jack shushed me with his fingers. He didn't think Aunt Emma would be pleased if I woke their baby. Aunt Emma hadn't finished yet though.

'I'm Chime,' she sang in a voice that was echo-close to mine, 'because I'm a Chime Child, born on Good Friday as the clock struck twelve.' She had her hands on her hips, and her head was held up high, as if she was a real proud Romany. I giggled. She could tongue-tease real well, could Aunt Emma. I had learned a lot from her.

'Just like we use our wagon names when none but our family can hear, so I would like to give Rose a wagon name, to show her that we're key-lock linked.'

'Does that mean we're family?' Aunt Emma asked, still teasing.

'Of course it does,' I told her seriously. 'Do you think that I would have told you my private name if you weren't heartbeat close?'

'So, what's the wagon name for our lovely Rose?' Aunt Emma and Uncle Jack asked together.

'Briar. She has to be a briar rose. She will grow

25

long-limbed, nature-beautiful. She will be deep-heart kind, and to make her fun, she'll be just a little bit wild and scratchy.'

'Well, that sounds like a pretty good combination to me,' Uncle Jack said quietly.

'And with all those qualities,' Aunt Emma added, 'she will be more than a bit like you.'

'I've brought her a present. Wait here, I'll be back in a moment.'

I raced across the landing to fetch my little patchwork bag. It had taken me absolutely hours to make. My hands had been finger-picking sore by the time I had finished. I won silver earrings for that! My great-gran had sworn that I'd never sit glue-stuck still, not for long enough to make it properly. My mam had known better. I'm too like my great-gran, I'm a pig-head stubborn one.

Maggie-Magpie was nosy-beak pleased to see me return to my room. I think my little bird-brained kackaratchi friend had been quite convinced that I had vanished for ever. She flew from her carry-bag perch by the window and landed on my shoulder to nibble my ear. Gently I shoved her away.

'I'm here to work magic, little one, and you can't come now. I have something important to do. Wait here, Kackaratchi.'

Maggie-Magpie flew back to her perch and I swear, open-hand honest, that she looked sag-bag sulky. I promised to tell her all about the baby when I returned. You have to do that, just like a beekeeper has to tell the bees when someone dies.

I hurried back to the nursery, clutching my bright little bag.

'Oh! That looks interesting,' Aunt Emma said. 'What have you got in there?'

'It has to be a secret until Briar Rose wakes.'

Uncle Jack gave the sleeping baby a gentle nudge. 'Well, I think that she had better wake now. I don't know about Em, but *I* am dying with curiosity.'

Briar Rose opened her eyes. They were wide and baby friendly. I gave her my very best smile, and I swear that she smiled straight back at me, even though I was strange to her. She smiled as her tiny fingers curled round my hand in welcome.

Reluctantly, I eased my hand free, so that I could dip into my stuffed-full stitched bag.

'I give you salt to savour,' I told Rose, saying with great care the words that my great-gran had taught me, when I was stumble-feet small. 'And bread for sustenance, and an egg so the Trinity will be with you, and matches to light your way.'

27

I sprinkled a tiny bit of salt on to my palm, and dipped in my little finger. Very, very, gently, I touched the baby's mouth with the crystal grains. Briar Rose screwed up her little heart-shaped mouth, but she didn't cry. In fact I think she looked at me wide-eyed curious. Her little tongue flicked like a scent-hunting snake.

'I give you salt to savour,' I repeated. 'May you taste life's riches, and know them for what they are.

'I give you bread for sustenance.' I broke off a small piece of bread, a bit so tiny that it couldn't cause choking. My great-gran had stressed that that was most important. It almost melted on her little pink tongue. 'May you never go hungry, may you never be in need.'

Briar Rose watched every move I made. It was like she understood that we were enchantment-linked.

By now, I was so busy making sure that I was doing things exactly right, that I quite forgot about Aunt Emma and Uncle Jack, even though they were standing close behind me.

'I give you this egg to touch with your hand.' I offered the egg that I had cleaned and boiled myself. 'An egg is made of three parts: the shell, the yolk and the white. These are joined together as one, just as the Trinity is made up of God, Jesus and the Holy Ghost. This Trinity is of great importance to you gorgios, and we respect them too, well, most of us.'

I paused for breath. That had been the hardest bit to get right. My great-gran had taught me best about our Romany gods, about Soster and Moshto and their three sons, and about how weighty they were to our living ways.

Great-gran said the creators are called different names by different people, so I was to trust the Trinity too, and any other deity that commanded nothing but love. It's how your heart is that is the most important thing of all.

I let Briar Rose hold on to the egg while I told her all this. 'I give you the Trinity egg, a reminder that your creator is always by your side.'

I was nearly through. I glanced at Aunt Emma and Uncle Jack. They were holding hands and I swear there were tickle-tears in their eyes. Grown-ups can be very sloppy sometimes. I turned back to look at Briar Rose.

'Finally, I give you matches to light your way.'

I carefully lit a match, and held it so that Briar Rose could see the flame. I held one of her fingers, gently but firmly, so that it couldn't slip. I touched her finger on to the white wood that carried the living fire. In the instant she touched the matchstick, the flame died. I was full-heart happy. I knew then that the living flame had passed into her heart.

'In the name of my people, I give you all these,' I said softly, kissing her forehead, 'and I give you too my own special wish. Baby Briar, I hope that you will carry along life's pathway a truly happy heart. May nothing trap you in sadness for long.'

It was over. My great-gran would be real proud when I told her all I had done, and how careful I had been to get it exactly right.

I carefully packed the remains of the dry bread, salt, matches and egg into the bag and gave it to Aunt Emma and Uncle Jack for safe keeping. They were big-beam smiling, and so was I. Briar Rose was now specially blessed, life should be good for her.

Even Briar Rose seemed pleased with my efforts. Her hands reached out to mine, and this time I sat for ages, letting my thumbs be held finger-hold tight. I felt as if Briar Rose could work magic too. Perhaps one day, when she's tongue-talk grown, we will work magic together. The very idea makes me sun-happy-faced.

5 Strawberry Woods

Mary is my best gorgio friend. Aunt Emma soon agreed that she should come and stay with us. I think she understood that, without Mary, I'd soon go hatter-mad with boredom. Aunt Emma and Uncle Jack would have people-filled their posh house to the very ceiling to try and help Penelope Bootle, they're that sort of people. Before long, Mary and I began to wonder why! Even on an outing it was obvious that Pouty Penny would be best left to drown in her own self-pity soup.

We sat in a row, Mary, Penny and me. Normally, Mary and I would have been excited about going to Strawberry Woods, but not today. It wasn't the same with Pudding Pot Penny tagging along. It wasn't the same at all!

For two days I'd tried to make friends with her, two endless-hour days. I'd pleaded and coaxed and begged, but Perverse Penny Bootle had just carried on staring into space and ignoring me. She'd been nothing but slap-shin rude.

I am a Chime Child but I am human too. Only two days have gone, but I am almost empty of patience. Like I said, Mary and I should have been sunshine-happy, but it was just not possible, not with Penny Bootle sat between us, looking every bit as exciting as a big sack of soggy potatoes.

'Do you think she'll like Strawberry Woods?' Mary asked, after yet another long silence.

'No,' I said, zipping up my carry bag so that the conductor wouldn't spot Maggie-Magpie, and charge me her fare.

'But it's beautiful.'

'Aunt Emma says that she's lost in sadness. Why, even when you came over to help, even then, she never bothered to say hello.' I leaned forward to whisper to Mary. 'Have you got the rucksack things?'

'Yes, tucked under the food.' Mary sighed. 'I feel so awkward, talking about her as if she isn't here.'

'How else can we talk? She's a dolt not to realise that you can't fight your destiny. I'm fed up with her behaving like a cardboard cut-out. I tell you, Mary, for the last two days I thought Old Father Time had turned up his toes.'

'My mum says he runs far too fast. She says that's how she knows she's getting old.'

'My great-gran swears he's lying in wait. She says he can lurk by her side all he likes. She's not giving up her vardo till she's good and ready.'

'Vardo?'

'The wagon I told you about. The one that I want, but has to be burned when she dies.'

'I reckon if you get Potty Penny Bootle talking, you'll have earned a palace, not an over-fancy cart.'

I paid our fares, and as soon as the bus conductor was safely gone I opened the carry bag so that Maggie-Magpie could see. 'Aunt Emma and Uncle Jack thought that an outing might cheer Penny up.'

'Well, I think it's useless to try,' Mary said, echoing the dark thoughts in my head. 'She might spoil Strawberry Woods for all of us.' I nodded agreement, and for a while the four of us stayed silent.

I am commanded to make Penny Bootle well yet, despite my best efforts, she stays damp-cloud dull, and does fat-pudding nothing. If I'm open-heart honest I feel like drowning her. I can't think of a single magic thing to do.

We climbed down from the bus at Henberry

Lane. Penny followed like a roly-poly puppy. She didn't smile, even though the air was honeysuckle fresh. She just trundled along behind us, with her nose pointing down to the back of our heels.

'At least she follows.'

'Yes, aren't we lucky!'

I wished that I had never seen her face in the dancing flames. I wished I was busy-bee herb gathering with my mam. I wished I was anywhere but here. It was hot. The world was wearing its bright blue biscuit-tin lid. We were quite glad to reach the welcoming green coolness of Strawberry Woods.

'The plan is still to go to Dewberry Pond . . . our plan?'

I nodded. The plan certainly wasn't Aunt Emma's.

'Will she be safe?' Mary glanced back at Penny, who never even raised her eyes, not even at the hint of danger. 'Can she really swim?'

'She's big enough,' I said, trying to sound more confident than I felt.

We entered the woods, and took the badger path that led straight to the pond. We were in a green sun-speckled box, kept cool from the heat of the day.

My spirit should be high in the trees, leaping

from branch to branch like my mutt-headed Magpie, not trapped in my gorgio shoes.

Dewberry Pond is huge. It's really more like a lake. In July the shallow end is so full of rushes, you can hardly tell the water is there, but in the deep end, the water is crystal clear and sweet for drinking. Mary and I love Dewberry Pond. It's peaceful and quiet, except sometimes on Sunday when the gorgio folk have family-day fun times. Even then it's not crowded, most gorgio folk find it too legging tired to make their way up the steep-way hill.

I expected Penny to be quite out of breath, but she wasn't. She wasn't anything . . . We made our way across to the deep-side end, stopping where a huge log hung right over the edge of the water. It was worn smooth by children climbing and fisher-men sitting. Ages and ages it had taken to wear the wood that smooth. My great-gran says the log is happiness-shined and, like her vardo carvings, living history is trapped inside. It's wonderful fun. When I last came, Mary and I spent hours here.

We hung our bags on a clothes-hook branch. I opened my carry bag wide, so Maggie-Magpie could see where she was to come back to. That done, Mary and I scrambled along the great log, holding on tight where we thought we might slip. We seated ourselves down at the very far end, our toes dipping down into the cold clear water. Then we waited to see what our great hulking shadow would do.

Just as Penny had never looked once at the waving pathside grasses, or at the shallow-side pond rushes, so she never glanced at the sun-speckled green-leaf roof, even though it set pretty lights dancing all over the shiny water. *She never even looked at the water!* No, Penelope Bootle just trolled along the log, acting for all the world as if it was a big main street, and plonked herself down beside us.

I was wordless! Even my dibby gran has more sense than that!

Mary shrugged her shoulders. 'She's a book short of a set.'

'Aunt Emma says she's really quite clever.'

'Aunt Emma would believe anything nice of anybody!'

Maggie-Magpie watched us from her carry-bag nest, all beady-eyed and knowing, like magpies are. When we were fairly settled, she decided it was time to play. She climbed up the strap, steadying herself with her beak, and when her feet were clear of the inside bag, she launched herself into flight.

'Your silly bird's escaping!' Mary warned.

I turned to look. Magpie gave me a squawk, and

flew away from our clearing and towards the deep wooded bit. Penny still stared unseeing, even when Maggie's blue-black wings shone like jewels in the brilliant sun. I wondered if she knew that she was missing out on such a shimmer-shine day.

'It's all right, Maggie-Magpie's free to go now any time she fancies. When we leave, she'll climb straight back into the bag, you see if I'm not right.'

Maggie-Magpie flew up on to a distant branch, and squawked at a local bird who was trying to oust her. My kackaratchi is a stroppy bird, *she* doesn't come second to *anybody*. The local magpie backed down, and sat sulky-faced on a branch nearby. Maggie-Magpie felt lion-heart victorious, and her frantic chattering bounced back and forwards through the whispering trees. Cross magpies can noise-shatter miles.

'Can't you gag that awful bird?'

'She likes a bit of fresh air, just like we do.'

For a moment, I imagined that I saw Penny's eyes follow the bird, but then I wasn't sure. Most likely, she was just staring straight ahead . . . as usual.

'I wonder what she's thinking. No, I wonder *if* she thinks?'

'Do you *really* want to know?'

'Well, it might *explain*.'

I wished I had an answer. I felt rag-doll wrung. Penny Bootle was pulling me into her mire. I smiled a brittle smile, and tried not to let my own scaredness show. We sat about for a while, waiting to see if Penny would do something . . . anything, but she didn't. We gave up, and set to our own enjoying.

'Time for our picnic,' I said, when we had spent more than an hour fishing, and had still caught nothing.

'I'd have done better with a jamjar!' Mary muttered, hauling in her line.

We weren't in the mood, and somehow the fish knew. You have to be in tune with nature, and we were all messed up over Penny.

Penny Bootle sat still, all lost in her miserable world. It was far too sunny for such sadness and, anyway, Mary and I were famished. We wondered if trundle-bundle Bootle was hungry too.

'Let's get the food!' I called, giving Mary my coded warning. 'Race you back to the clothes-hook tree.'

I started as if I was going to race along the branch. I tried to move as if it was smooth-plank flat.

'Be careful!' Mary warned, more scared of deep

water than me, but I took no heed. I slipped, of course! I slipped straight into the puddle-brained Penny. She teetered for a moment, but my falling was too strong. We touch-tumbled down, straight into cold clear water.

Even I gasped. The water was far colder than I had believed, its deepness unwarmed by the leaf-filtered sun. Penny, however, made no sound. She didn't cough or splutter or scream. She just floated like a giant cork, not caring what happened. She never even sucked in her mouth with shiver-shock!

'Are you all right?' I screamed, frantic to get her answering. She didn't even look up.

Things were not going to plan, by now Penny Bootle should be calling out in anger or fear, not bobbing about turning chill-skin blue. Desperate for help, I summoned Magpie, but even when Maggie-Magpie dive-bombed her head she stayed all expressionless, and a kackaratchi's flapping can usually make *anyone* scream . . .

'*Come on! Swim to me.*'

Penny floated almost motionless, like an abandoned letter-bottle. Her legs still, despite the freezing water. She didn't, as I had imagined, look at me with her depths-of-despair eyes before calling for help, neither did she panic. I swear she seemed almost pleased at the chance of drowning. She drifted about, a solitary soul in an eternal sea.

'*In the name of Soster, please do something*!' I yelled, but still Penny did nothing, her mouth simply dipped a little closer to the water. I gave up. I reached out and grasped her hand.

As I touched her, a thinking shock went through me. Just for a moment, I felt her emotion. Penny's head was full of cold blind fury. She felt I had let her down, stopped her from joining Katya!

'It's not your time,' I told her gently, before dragging her back to Mary, who was waiting at the side of the bank.

Mary and I leaf-scrubbed Penny dry. Mary produced the spare clothes we had hidden in the rucksack and helped her to change. I lit a fire for warmth and tea. Soon we were warm and fat-tummy full, even Penny. She wasn't difficult to manage. If you put something into her hand she ate it, showing no pleasure and no disgust: onions, chocolate, bread, anything.

'Why did you give her a *worm*? That was a bit mean!' Mary said, watching Penny mechanically chewing her food.

'Well, I don't suppose you'll believe me, but it

was an accident. I meant to give it to Maggie, but I got my hands mixed up.'

Mary shrugged. She didn't really care whether it was an accident or not, and neither did I. Why should we? It didn't bother Penny Bootle.

It was as if the pond-falling had never happened. We ate our picnic in the sunshine. We drank our orange and waited patiently for our baked potatoes to blacken nicely. Only the clothes drying on the shrubbery gave a clue to the fact that Penny and I had got wet at all.

'Well, that plan was a total failure!' Mary said grumpily. 'What on earth are you going to try now?'

'Do you really have to go home tonight?' I asked Mary, dreading the idea of her leaving.

'It's my sister Antonia's birthday tomorrow, and I have to go to the dentist on Friday.' Mary gave me her most impish grin. 'Even going to the dentist has got to be better than being stuck with her! Oh yes, Freya! I'm going home.'

My face fell. I needed Mary. She was like a spring day after winter. I could never manage the problem Penny alone. Again I wished I had never stared into those dancing flames, never seen those black eyes calling. 'You will come back?' I sounded pit-stomach desperate. I, who should be high-head Romany proud.

Mary gave me a hug. 'I'm your friend, little gypsy, of course I'll come back.'

I sighed with relief. Somehow I knew that I needed Mary, as much as Penelope Bootle needed me.

6 Problems

'Poor Norman,' Aunt Emma was saying. 'What with all that running about, it's no wonder that he looks so tired.'

I stood in the doorway, all ready to be kissed goodnight. They didn't notice, they were too busy being all concerned.

'He's so upset he's not eating properly either,' Uncle Jack told Aunt Emma. 'That's why I was so late home. I took him some of your casserole. He said he was late and couldn't stop, so I left it on a low light. He can eat it when he gets home.'

'Who's Norman?' I asked, all poky-nose curious, as soon as they spotted me.

'You're earwigging again, Freya!' Aunt Emma's tone was scolding.

'No, I wasn't! You never saw me, that's all. Who's Norman?'

'Norman is my younger brother,' Uncle Jack said, 'and he's almost as nice as me.' Uncle Jack winked at me. 'But not quite . . . you see, only one of us can be perfect.'

'Can I meet him then?'

'Well, I expect you'll meet him soon, but he's very busy just now.' Uncle Jack gave me a kiss, and so did Aunt Emma. 'So, off you go to bed, little Romany. Have sweet dreams, and leave us to worry about feeding Norman. Don't wake Penelope, will you? She went to sleep simply hours ago.'

Uncle Jack had made his voice teasing, but I knew he was wrinkle-worried. If Uncle Norman was nearly as nice as Uncle Jack, then I hoped he wasn't as sick as Pudding Pot Penny.

I made my way quietly into the bedroom, and sat by the open window.

Maggie flew to my shoulder, even though it was only just light enough for her to see. I had been so busy with Penny Bootle that she must have felt quite neglected. She sat on my shoulder and grumbled softly as I scratched her head.

The sky was dressed with a blue-black tinge, and once my eyes were dark-adapted, I could see quite clearly. A vixen fox crept out of the shrubbery with her second brood. She stood guard, while they gambolled on Aunt Emma's regulation lawn. The little family sniffed the soldier flowers, looking for worms and slugs. I'm sure not a single one was there. I hoped Uncle Jack hadn't planted poisonous pellets that could harm them.

The fox mother sensed I was watching. She looked straight up at the window. She was wary of folk in gorgio houses. She gave a little warning cry to her cubs, and led them back down to the safety of the wild garden. I was pleased, there would be plenty of frogs to eat there.

Penny called out in her sleep, and waved her arms in fear. I raced to her and, despite knocking her bed in my haste, she didn't fully wake.

'Sh . . . Sh. All *will* be well,' I whispered.

Penny moaned and turned over in her fitful sleep. I held her hand until she calmed. Poor Penny, it wasn't *her* fault that Katya had been killed. It was time she stopped blaming herself, time to start living.

I went back to the window and sat there, rubbing Maggie's head. I couldn't sleep. Too many things were going wrong. Uncle Norman wasn't getting time to eat, Penny Bootle wouldn't talk, and Maggie and I, we yearned to be night-time free. Yes, I had troubles enough of my own. Aunt Emma and Uncle Jack had such faith in me, yet all my magic was wild-windswept gone.

I had to show Penny I cared but I didn't know how. Somehow, I had to discover how to make her better, only then could I go home. Even looking out of the window made me heart-sink homesick. My gran is as dibby as dumplings but sometimes, just sometimes, I envy her. She will go through a whole lifetime mostly happy. She has the least worries of us all.

I put Maggie gently back on her carry-bag perch and kissed her goodnight. I still wasn't tired, just stone-prison-house weary. Reluctantly, I crept back to my bed.

I tossed and turned, unable to escape from the hot sticky night-time room. At home I could ignore my bed in Mam's big shiny caravan and creep out. My mam pretends not to hear. She knows a Chime Child is pure wild Romany, not half house gorgio, and so perfectly safe. I usually go to my great-gran's vardo. I love to curl up warm and safe between the great wooden wheels, with Fusty, Sabre and Woodpile to keep me warm. I never shiver-shake, not even in the cold mists of morning. Dogs are wonderful body-warmers.

When I was toddle-foot small, my mam used to frizzle-fret. 'She'll come to no harm,' my great-gran had reminded her constantly. 'She's chosen.'

Eventually, my mam had relaxed, and now she simply lets me be.

My heart felt soggy-sad, my family seemed far away, and my tummy butter-mix-frothed. Even telling Maggie about my day failed to make me feel good. Anyway, Maggie had stopped listening, her head was tucked up under her wing, and she was fast asleep. Sometimes her manners are as poor as those of Penelope Bootle.

I pulled from under my pillow, our big family crystal. Once, long ago, it had lots of shiny faces that were cut like diamonds. Now it was worn smooth like a clear teardrop pebble. My mam, and my great-gran, said it was worn smooth with love. It helped me mind-think home, especially when my mind was stacked up stumble-stewed.

Suddenly I *was* safe under the vardo, peeking out at the twinkly stars with Fusty, Sabre and Wood-pile. They were cuddled up close so the morning damp didn't even kiss my nearly sleeping bones.

A mist-dew muddle-brain I am, yet I am a Chime Child too. Magic is my very being. Why is it, then, that the answer to Penny's problems won't come?

'*You have to work at it*!' My great-gran's voice

rang clear in the silence of the night. 'Nothing comes easy in life, Freya, you should know that.'

'But I can't think of *anything*, Gran.'

'Well then, at this moment you're little more than useless ... even if your heart does hold a nugget of gold.'

I sat bolt upright in my hot sticky house bed. My great-gran was wonderful. She always helped, always, always. She had sent me a clue, and the clue was gold.

Next morning, I told my plan to Aunt Emma and Uncle Jack. They were not happiness-shaped! Not at all.

'You can't go, Freya. It's just too dangerous.'

'But we must. You said yourself, we have to try *everything*.'

'No!' said Aunt Emma.

'No!' said Uncle Jack.

'You *have* to let us go.' I was beyond pleading. I was telling them a simple truth.

'No!' said Aunt Emma, but then a bit of doubt flitted across Uncle Jack's face. 'Well, maybe,' he said, 'if it's really that important. I'll have a small word with Aunt Emma in private.' He led her out of the room for their grown-up talk. I was hot horse-frothing mouthed while I waited. He had to let us go!

I paced round and round the room while I waited. I thought that I would wear out the carpet pattern with my ever-treading feet. Eventually, when my tummy was truly tumble-mixed, they came back.

'You promise not to separate . . . not even for a moment?'

I nodded.

'You promise to be as quick as you can?'

I nodded again.

'Just three mornings?'

'Just three.'

'I'll give you a big warning whistle. You must blow it if you even sense a hint of trouble.'

'Of course, Uncle Jack.' I gave him my most serious nodding face, and stood as grown-up tall as I could. 'I promise.'

He smiled, but Aunt Emma still looked very worried. Her hands were clenched tight into fists, her lips string-thin pinched.

'And I won't even look at a stranger,' I added, hoping to ease her mind.

'Please, God, let there be no strangers,' Aunt

Emma muttered as she left the room. It was obvious that she was not best pleased with Uncle Jack.

Before we went to bed, I led Penny into the kitchen, and settled her down in her chair. I sat right opposite her and called her name. As usual, she ignored me.

I took her head in my hands, and forced her to look towards my eyes, even though I was not sure what she chose to see, she with the bored senseless eyeballs that had lost all their living glitter.

'Listen here, Penelope Bootle. Nobody gets given anything for nothing. My great-gran insists on that. Now I want something very much, and you are going to help me to get it.'

Penny ignored me, not even bothering to turn away.

'You have to help me, Penny. Uncle Jack says I can't go alone. Anyway you *have* to come with me, and you will do as you are told.'

It was like talking to a pillow. My emotion-mind wanted to slap her vicious hard, beat her even more soggy-senseless. I wanted to hit her pudding face until she cried and cried and cried. I had struggled so hard to be nice, only wanting to help, to be her friend, but it was so difficult when she never even tried.

Slowly I counted ten and back again. There was no point in hitting her. She was indifferent to everything. I was supposed to be calm and strong. I was expected to make her better. I had been called. I had no choice but to help.

I gritted my teeth and explained my plan. 'Penelope Bootle, I shall drag you out of bed when it's almost light. We will walk, as fast as we can, to the little common at Endall Place. Do you understand? You will most definitely come, even if I have to haul you every step of the way.'

Penny didn't move, not even a muscle twitched.

Now if someone had told me that I had to get up in the depths of night and walk down two whole streets to an empty common, I would not more do it than fly! And I'm a Romany girl, not an overprotected gorgio kid. I'm used to darkness hours and open spaces, but even I never creep off at night, especially with someone who's almost a stranger. Not even Maggie would come. No, the kackaratchi has a mind to stay wing-tucked sleeping, like the bubbo, Briar Rose.

'*I mean it, Penny! I shall be here to collect you when it's nearly morning, and you just have to come!*'

Penny's empty eyes looked out from her inside

space. She never uttered a single word. Oh, how hard it was to be kind. More than a bit of me still wanted to smash sullen Pudding Face to sludge!

7 The Joining

'Come on!'

I stood itchy-foot impatient, while Penny climbed into her clothes. She was doing as she was told but at the speed of an old arthritic snail. She dressed without smiling or talking, yet showed no sign of sandman sleepiness. It was as if she had no head-thinks at all.

As we were just about to leave the room I spotted a handkerchief bundle neatly placed by Penny's bedside lamp. 'Is that made of silk?' I asked.

Penny didn't answer so I went to look for myself, pulling open the ends of the baby pink ribbon holding the bundle shut. Just for an instant Penny's eyes met mine, but she didn't offer a single whisper-whimper, even though her fingers curled into a fist just as Aunt Emma's had done, when I had told her about my plan. Penny was obviously even more anxious than usual, so the little bundle was important to her.

Inside the lace-edged hanky was a baby dummy and an old silver sixpence. The sort that most grannies insist on placing in plum puddings for luck, and some mothers give as presents for new-born babies. I put the dummy and the sixpence very carefully by the lamp, and Penny's hands relaxed a bit, even though I hung on to the hanky. It *was* made of real silk. My heart felt hippy-hoppy happy. It belonged to Penny, so would make far better magic than the one I had borrowed from Aunt Emma.

When Penny was full-frock ready, I folded the silk square neatly and handed it over. 'Hold your handkerchief carefully. It's very important.'

Penny's fingers tightly clenched in an instant. It was clear that she had no intention of losing her silver-sixpence silk wrap.

We crept out of the house, being very careful not to wake up Aunt Emma or Uncle Jack. I gripped Penny's free hand, and dragged her along the silent streets as fast as I could. I wished Maggie had come too, but she was a stubborn feather-head, determined not to stir even though there was a faint hint of morning.

The streets were edged in a pale eerie light. Morning mist hung like silver cobwebs in the air. I breathed in deeply, sucking the pre-dawn coldness deep into my lungs. The taste was tingle-tongue sweet. I love this hazy morning time. It's moody and mighty magical.

All around us stood sleepy-time houses. Nothing stirred, not even a morning town fox intent on a dustbin raid. I felt shiver-shake nervous. There was me and Penny, *and* the dawn of morning, yet I felt more lonely than I did when I walked through the night alone. I hurry-scurried us, and in no time at all we reached Endall Common.

I led Penny over to the long-size grass. It was still only just light enough to see. Dancing night-time shadows flickered carelessly. The grass was delicate dew-fresh wet and I was mightily pleased to see it. It could be that things were going well at last.

'Give me your silk handkerchief, Penny.'

Penny obeyed as if she had nothing to lose. It didn't make sense, her fingers uncurling when her brain should surely tell her different.

I took the lace-lined silk that was far too pretty to use, and laid it down on the dew-kissed grass, so the hanky could soak up its wetness.

Penelope Bootle was a sick-head child! Would you let a strange gypsy girl steal your treasure and get it spoiled? No, of course you wouldn't, but

Penny did. Penny never said a word. She might be silent-stubborn but she could have *tried* to stop me.

When the hanky was soggy-soaked damp, I pulled from my hand the plain gold ring that my great-great-gran had given me soon after my birth, on the day she'd chosen for passing on to the happy lands.

'Old to young. New from old,' she'd said, watched by my great-gran, my mam, and my dibby gran. She'd removed the gold ring from her knobby-knuckled hand, kissed it, and placed it in my palm. My fingers had curled, exactly like those of Briar Rose. In that moment I took possession of not just the ring, but my family's past and, hopefully, its future. The whole tribe had gathered. Some had come from far across country, some by wagon, others on foot, or by horse. They had gathered without a word being spoken, no patteran had been laid. Somehow each and every one had known the passing time had come. They had gathered as they always do, to honour my great-great-gran's leaving, and to acknowledge my arrival. The family needed to see the life-line safely passed through the ring. They watched and joyously noted. Great-great-gran was still smiling as she died.

My mam had threaded the ring on a ribbon and

pinned it to my clothes. Later, when I was stumble-feet tall I wore it as a necklace. Now, at last, I wear it on my finger. Old to young. New from old. The ring, like our crystal, is heart-magic full. I am the chosen one, a Chime Child, who can properly use these things.

I threaded Penny's dew-wet handkerchief through the ring. I did it three times, just like my great-gran had shown me when she led me through the wondrous ways of magic.

Three mornings, and three passings on each morning. That added up to nine bathings. Nine is a number of importance. Hopefully, it will help cure eyes that choose not to see.

Carefully I pulled the delicate silk through the gold ring, and then brushed the damp material against Penny's dull dead eyes.

'This silk is a link,' I said on the first passing, almost relieved that Penny didn't have the tongue-speak, to turn my tummy-tremble butterflies into big batty bats.

'This ring is a joining,' I told her the second time I tugged the fine silk through.

'This touching is a bond between you and me,' I recited, dragging the silk for the third and last time that morning. Penny Bootle didn't even look at me as if I was stark-mad stupid.

I slipped the ring back on to my finger and put the damp handkerchief back in her hand. Her fingers closed, but apart from that, there was no reaction at all. I took her by the hand and led her back home. She was still a useless pudding pile.

The second morning was almost the same except that Penny wouldn't hurry and, just as we reached the end of our street, I thought I heard footsteps. I stopped us both still, and kept so quiet that we barely breathed. My ears were all silence-filled. There was no sound, nothing at all. I was catching gorgio nervousness. I was becoming shadow-scared. I was losing the strength of me.

The magic was started so I had no choice but to continue. I led Penny over to the longest grass. It was harder this time to dampen her flimsy silk. The night had been hot, and already the dewness was nearly gone. I had to dab about for ages to catch the morning damp.

'This silk is a link,' I said, passing the handkerchief silk through my family gold ring for the first time, before brushing Penny's eyes.

'This ring is a joining,' I chanted, desperately

hoping that the tiny bit of wetness was enough to work the magic.

'And this touching is a bond between you and me.'

Penny blinked, but that was all she did. I gave her handkerchief back and hurried her home. To make the magic you have to believe, and that was a deep-pit problem for Pudding Pot Penny.

On the third morning, it was even more difficult to make Penny climb into her clothes. She was stuck-stubborn slow, her full face scowly. It wasn't until we were ready to leave that she gave in and followed along, and that was because even she was sure that that way my foolishness would fastest be over.

I heard footsteps again, this time just as we reached the common. I closed my eyes and let my whole body help with the listening. I was sure there was somebody there, but I heard only scary-whisper leaves, and in the shadows I couldn't see.

I fingered Uncle Jack's big whistle, and hurried Penny over to the tall grasses as fast as I could.

The night had been properly behaved. Great big droplets hung on the tall grass whisper-heads like dew-drop pearls. They looked far too beautiful to touch. Reluctantly I wetted Penny's fine silk, which was by now more than a fair bit grubby. While I worked my magic I tried not to hear the rustlings in the bushes that were beginning to sound full scary unfriendly.

'This silk is a link.' I concentrated hard, ignoring the swelling sound behind me and putting on my best believing voice, as I pulled the hanky through the ring as fast as I could, before dabbing Penny's eyes.

'This ring is a joining.' I tried to give the words their proper significance, but say them at gobble-goose speed.

The bush noises were sounding ever closer. They were not fox, and they certainly weren't rabbit. I tried not to let fear swamp my mind. I *had* to finish the magic. I was so nearly through. I couldn't let *anything* spoil it now.

'This touching is a bond between you and me,' I told Penny firmly, dabbing her eyes for the third and last time, on the third and last morning.

The bush sounds were neck-tingle close. I turned and, now the morning was nearly light and bright enough to banish most of the night's shadows, I was sure I could see the shape of a creeping man. A man who thought he was stealthy-silent, a hunter.

'Hurry, Penny,' I whispered. 'Hurry, please. It's really important.'

For a moment, Penny held my gaze, then we started to run, and as we raced to the safety of the newly lighted streets, I felt Penny's fingers clamp tightly round my hand.

We were running mighty fast. I tried to make Penny think I was playing a game, that the running was part of the magic. I don't think she had spotted the man, or understood the danger, but I did. The shadow man, with the very long legs was rapidly shortening the gap between us.

I grabbed my big whistle, making sure it was ready to use. I even pulled it up to my lips but I just couldn't bring myself to blow. Deep down I felt winter-white-faced frightened. The man in the shadows was coming closer and closer. I was tied-tongue terrified, but determined not to let it show.

'Come *on*, Penny. Surely you can run as fast as me?'

I felt grateful that she couldn't argue. '*Come on*, slowcoach,' I goaded, pulling her firmly by the arms and ignoring the sound of her heaving lungs. The shadow man was rapidly closing the gap between us.

Penny Bootle was already full-heart scared from

sadness. If I blew my whistle to call for help it would frighten her even more. I couldn't do that. I *couldn't* let her realise I was faint-heart scared, for both of us.

After what seemed like for ever we reached the line of street houses. I slipped down the side of the first bulb-lit house, pulling Penny close behind me. I tucked us both into the shelter of the side porch, ready to ring the bell if the shadow man came too close.

We stood huddled together, both of us gasping for breath. 'You ran real well,' I whispered to Penny. 'Now you have to keep as quiet as you can.' I felt silly telling a dumb girl not to talk, but I was still trying to make her believe that all we had done was play Let's Pretend.

As the thumping in my heart slowed, I could hear the shadow man was panting too. He glanced down by the side of the house as he drew close, but couldn't see us. I sighed in relief. He was probably thinking we were somewhere ahead.

I stared at the man as he passed. In the light of the front window I could see his face clearly. I felt an explosion of hot-head angryness. The shadow man who had scared us half to death was Uncle Jack!

Trying to appear calm, I led Penny home. Her

fingers were willingly curled into mine but I was so cross I barely noticed. Penny glanced at me with her great sad brown eyes before clutching even harder on to my hand. I felt muddle-stomach mixed up. I was angry with Uncle Jack, and sad and disappointed that the ring magic hadn't worked, all at the very same time. Mostly though, I was wild shaking mad.

'You followed us!' I accused him as soon as we burst through the door. 'You followed us and scared us half to death!'

'Of course I followed you!' Uncle Jack retorted. 'Two young girls wandering about in the middle of the night. Did you really think that I could let you go alone?'

I glared at him all wordless, then stomped upstairs to tell Maggie about Uncle Jack spoiling things. I explained how the joining magic had failed despite all my best efforts. The only good thing that I could think of to talk-tell was, all being well, Mary would be back tomorrow.

8 Morning Magic

Just before the morning gets up is a magic time. The creatures of the night have tucked up ready for the sandman, and the sun-happy things are still wrapped in sleepy black folds.

I love this nowhere time. I feel like it is especially mine.

Mary and Penny lie sandman sleeping. Mary's red hair is tumble-twisted all over her pillow, making a striking frame for her freckle-speckle face. She's snoring so gently that you can only just hear, but she *is* snoring. Mary is never keen on long-time quiet. I love Mary, she's the nicest gorgio girl I know, and not just because she's giving up her holiday to help me with Penny.

Maggie and I creep past their beds, being careful not to wake folk who think that lunch-time is heartbeat-close to morning.

Penny doesn't really sleep. Hers is a night-time chaos. She tosses this way and that, her arms flail, and her face is twisted by the ghosts of the night. She drives me mad! I can't say I love her, but I don't really hate her. She mixes up my think-thoughts until I'm giddy with their endless spinning. I want to give her back the simple joy of living. Until that is done I cannot go home. Penny whimpers. I leave Maggie by the window and take hold of her nail-bitten hands. 'It *will* end, Pen,' I whisper. 'I will stay until the magic is right, and so will Mary. You *will* be well-minded again.'

Maybe she hears me. Her body calms and her breathing slows. Satisfied that all is well, I open the door. Little shafts of light creep in from the hall. Maggie-Magpie wants company and flies to my shoulder. Quietly, we slip out of the room. Maggie's cautious-silent now, for outside is creep-shadow land, but all too soon she will nag us all to death with her early morning chattering.

This is my time to find the bubbo, Briar Rose. It's easiest now for us all. I can play with her without upsetting Penny, and we can cultivate our special bonding, one that one day will cross time and space, needing no silks or fine gold rings. For the moment though, we simply share the delights of the dawning, this bubbo and I.

I lift Briar Rose from her fancy-frill cot, and

hold her comfy-close. She opens her eyes and smiles. I take her to the window so she too can smell and taste the birth of morning. The air is echo-air soundless. I stand with Briar Rose in my arms, and Maggie-Magpie on my shoulder. We are all as secret silent as this time-change space. We have each other, and that is everything we need. Little Rose turns her face to the window so I open it wide. Briar Rose gurgles in delight as she's kissed by the sleepy mists of morning. Outside is losing its blackness. We watch trees and bushes grow out of lumps in the shawls of grey. Nothing stirs. It's like time itself has stopped.

We wait as we've done most mornings now. The first time, I expected baby Rose to spoil things, but so far she never ever has.

The grey-blanket sky is changing its dress to a rising frill of pink. It's beautiful. Rolling hills are best for this sort of morning, all the waves of earth change colour, growing ever warmer with the rising sun. Autumn, though, is the very best time of all, for then Jack Frost leaves little fingers of glistening white, and even these can be changed to twinkle-pink. Today is still summer. Even though the air holds a hint of chill it smells fresh-grass warm. I suck in my breath, and sweetness fills my lungs, my must-you-hear-everything ears register tiny chirps. The silent time is over. More and more chirping celebrates the greeting of the day. They are truly chatter-bird cheerful, the air is full of their busy-beak sounds. Far down the road, a car coughs and splutters. A distant baby cries.

Maggie stretches her wings and her feet, right side, left side, slowly, carefully. She nudges up close and nibbles my ear. She doesn't wait to hear me whisper good morning. She flies out, eager to make her mark on the bright new day. She's a kackarat-chi, born to be bossy blue-black noisy. I laugh at her haste to go, and so does my baby Briar.

'I don't really like babies,' I tell Briar Rose. 'They're noisy and smelly and uninteresting. Maggie might be squarky, but she's full of feather-fun.'

Little Rose smiles, and reaches out to clasp my nose.

'But you're different, little Briar. If it wasn't for Penny I'd talk to you more often. You're a bit special. I think *you* understand what it's like to be *me*.'

Baby blue eyes stare into mine. We've been together ages, yet she still hasn't made an unhappy sound. The baby down the road is shriek-siren

67

wailing. I'm glad my Briar Rose is not like that! I tuck her back into her cot, being careful to make sure she's warm and safe, and blow her a kiss as I leave. I'm glad my mam can't see me. She'd think me real gorgio soft, fussing a bubbo so. Briar Rose is a mul-sko-dud, a will-o'-the-wisp. Aunt Emma and Uncle Jack are right, she's more than a bit like me.

I open the front door, not making a sound, and let myself out. The air is day-tingle-burst new and wonderful fresh. The wild garden draws me. It's the only place that is a little bit like home. Maggie will find me, and we will wait there until the gorgios are finally ready to admit it's morning.

I look tough-face normal, but I feel heart-hungry homesick. I'm so glad Mary is back. I don't think I could cope with Pudding Pot Penny any more, not alone. This magic has to succeed, but I think it needs Mary, Magpie, and me.

9 The Picnic

'Don't just sit there, Penny! Go and gather some firewood.'

I knew that I was being scratchy-tongued irritable but, sometimes, I wish that I had never done the joining magic. Penny Bootle and me are glue-stuck joined now. Maggie-Magpie is swooping and diving, and I'm green-eye-filled envious. I long to be sitting on a log in the middle of the forest, or gathering watercress by a distant stream. I yearn for a small respite of loneliness.

We're supposed to be happy campers, but wherever I am, there is Penny, grasping my hand or just sitting so close that I feel I cannot properly breathe. Even Maggie-Magpie thinks we're joined. Now she sits on both of us. I would be happy if Penny would talk, but she doesn't. She just wide-eye lingers. She's real draggy-feet dumb.

'Penny, it's *your* turn to gather firewood!'

Mary and I gasped in surprise. Penny not only

did as she was told, she went willingly, all by herself, to look for firewood. 'I'll help her,' Mary offered. 'I haven't got the knack of turf cutting anyway.' I nodded, pleased at the chance to be at one with myself.

I took out my long knife. The one that my brother, Tashar, had made just for me. Last time I'd stayed with Aunt Emma and Uncle Jack, my mam had made me leave my knife in the vardo. 'Gorgios don't understand! Some of them is stupid with knives, so they thinks they are dangerous,' she'd warned. This time was different. 'She trusts you now, Chime, she knows you'll only use it proper.'

Carefully I cut out a big square of turf. The weather had been hot and dry for days. If we'd just lit a fire any old ways, we'd have burned the field and more. I stacked the cut turfs in the shade of the hedge. We would have ourselves fun, replace the clods, and, in two days, it would seem as if we had never been.

The day was warm-summer wonderful. Once my cooking space was stripped bare, I lay on my back by the edging grass, sucking out the sweetness of a freshly plucked stalk. Cotton-wool clouds popped about now and then, but mostly the sky was plain cornflower blue.

Mary and Penny were taking a long time wood gathering. Maggie-Magpie had gone with them. I guess she thought things would be more exciting in the woods. She's getting go-far brave now, my kackaratchi.

It was nice not to be in hurry-time. This was a great-to-be-alive moment. I watched the fluffy clouds, skipping about like little lost lambs, playing in an azure ocean instead of a fresh green field, not enough to shadow-spoil things, but sufficient to make the sky interesting.

It was the sort of day where, back at our stopping place, my mam would be drying her specially gathered herbs, laying and turning, until they were perfectly ready for use.

Her mum, my dibby gran, would be skipping and singing all day. Mark you, she is always sunshine-happy, even if it's rain-wet drenching! She's lovely, my dibby gran, sometimes I think it's *because* she has the mind of a tiny child.

In my mind-thinks, I could hear Great-gran who, of course, would be sitting on her vardo steps bossing the whole world, like she always does.

'Tashar, you're making that leading rein far too long! Do you want to be for ever poor? What sort of

Rom are you, selling such fine leather at such a snatch-from-your-hand price?'

'Don't nag, Ostrich!' Tashar would say, using the wagon name that we young ones were not supposed to even whisper, well, not without fear of a tongue lashing because we could be thought rude.

'I tell you, that strap is far too long. Didn't your great-grandpa learn you nothing?'

Even my biggest brother, Vashti, would not escape. 'And just because you're putting in a guest appearance, you needn't think you can grin. All that junk you have, and where's your fortune?'

Tashar would simply laugh, but Vashti would sigh, and threaten to go off travelling again with his new young wife, anywhere he could get some peace. Great-gran would light her clay pipe and puff out great big white clouds of crossness, but after all that, nothing would change. The leading rein would stay long. Vashti would only travel when the mood really took him and Great-gran would fill the air with grumbles. Mam would continue to gather herbs, and none of us would go far from the others for more than a few short moons. We didn't need a silk and gold joining. To us, any Romany is family, and the family is never *really* apart.

My mouth grass felt dry. I'd fair sucked out all

its sweetness. I opened my eyes so as to hunt myself out another.

'Well, hello, lazy-bones!' Mary said, dumping a pile of dry branches into my dry earth space. 'I always *knew* that gypsies were born bone-idle!'

I would have thumped her even though she was my friend, but her eyes were like twinkle-stars, and her voice full of bubble-burst laughter, so I shoved her gently away instead.

Penny Bootle stood before me, her arms laden with an even bigger pile than Mary's. It was so high that you could only just see her nose. Maggie-Magpie sat right on top of her head. It was the only place she could fit. Penny's dark eyes held a hint of warmth and pride, there was even a touch of colour in her cheeks. Perhaps the joining was working after all.

'Well, Penny! That's wonderful!' I told her, rewarding her with a hug and a gorgio kiss. 'Penny Bootle, you must have worked *very hard indeed*.'

Penny smiled as I took the great pile of wood and put it safe to one side. It was only a little smile, but it was a proper one that crinkle-spread to her eyes.

I made a small pad of dry grass. It's best to start a fire small. I added a bundle of fine twigs and blew gently, until my flames were tongue-lick gold, then, when it was great-stretch flaming and full-bonfire happy, I added the big logs, making sure that I chose them first from Penny's pile. Within minutes we had a fire, one that any Romany would have been proud to sit beside.

'I'm famished. What are we going to eat?' Mary asked. Mary is amazing, she can eat anything she wants and still stay bean-pole slim.

'Potato-sweet.'

'What, cheese and potato?'

'No! Like I told you, potato-sweet. It's mouth-water tasty. We always have it for treats, especially when there's young ones about, like your brother, Jamie.'

'But we're not babies!'

'You like sweet things, don't you?'

'Not if they're for babies, I don't!'

I sighed. 'I said young ones, not babies . . . are you old?'

'No.'

'Are you of spread-tummy middle years?'

'Don't be stupid.'

'Then we eat potato-sweet.'

'But . . .'

'Listen, when I wanted to catch and roast us a

rabbit, you went and uggy-aghed! You suddenly wanted nice ham sandwiches, you even knew Aunt Emma would cut the crusts off, but that's not proper fun, is it? So you can choose. We have pot-roast bunny, or potato-sweet.'

'You couldn't catch a rabbit!'

'Watch me!'

Mary and I stared eye to eye. Penny mouth-gaped. She sensed I was into a serious daring. She never said a word, but she really watched.

'We'll have potato-sweet,' Mary said at last, and again Penny really smiled.

I put the potatoes into the fire to bake. When they were halfway done, I would make them taste lip-smacking good.

While they were baking, we found ourselves some daisies to make into chains. Penny watched, but this time she didn't join in. She sat comfy-close, all the time coiling and uncoiling a strand of grass.

Mary and I chose ourselves flowers with nice thick stalks.

'Once there was nothing,' I said, threading a buttercup stalk through a slit I had made with my nail in another.

'Nothing?'

'Not a thing . . . anywhere. No earth, no sky, no people.'

'Oh!' said Mary. 'You mean before the world began.'

I waited until she stopped cursing because she had split her stem slit with her far-too-long nails. When she'd picked a fresh daisy, I started again.

'Out of the nothingness came fire. The fire grew bigger and bigger and bigger. One day it blew right up! There was a huge explosion of fire, and out of that fire, two great gods were born.'

Mary rested her head on her bent-up knees. She loves stories, especially living legends, even Penny seemed interested, her sad face half-turned towards mine.

'Those two gods, born out of flames, are the great gods of Romany life.'

'How do you know?'

'The knowing was passed on to us by the prophet Soster.'

Mary grinned. She placed her daisy-chain over Penny's head, and started another. Penny took no notice of the delicate little flowers, she was too busy watching me.

'The two gods were Moshto, who is the god of life, and Arivell, the god of death. To be trusty-mouth truthful, you cannot have one without the other.'

'Oh, like Jesus and Satan?'

'No! These are proper Romany gods; everybody can share yours!'

'Well, they seem about the same to me,' Mary muttered as she threaded a really fat daisy.

'No, they're different. Moshto had *three* sons and all of his sons have a really important job to do.'

'What jobs?'

'The eldest son has to go right on creating life.'

'Oh! He's in charge of the gooseberry bush,' Mary said, giggling at her very own joke. I ignored her.

'The second son, well, he's more like a mechanic. He must keep the life-stream going.'

'Like a gardener?' Mary said, more seriously, 'Or a doctor?'

I nodded. 'And the third son, well, he has the most difficult job of all. He has to do something that most of us would hate to do.'

'Go on! Tell us.'

'Well, he has to destroy any part of the life-stream that endangers the rest. Sometimes he might even have to destroy some people in order to save others. Life is not easy for him, sometimes it's nail-bite frightening, having to choose what to do.'

'Like pest control, or crime prevention?'

I nodded. 'Yes, or like guard bees dying to defend their hive, or isolating people with the plague. He has to try and make sure that the proper-progression things aren't spoiled.'

'We had a Garden of Eden once,' Mary told me, putting an even longer chain round Penny's neck. 'I suppose that was spoiled because we didn't have a son of Moshto to stop Eve tempting Adam with the apple.'

'I'm not sure,' I admitted, not understanding how a garden was spoiled if only one apple was eaten. I supposed the gorgio God must like his garden even more tidy than Uncle Jack's. 'Anyway, it's the god Arivell who gives Penny her nightmares, not Moshto's third son. It's Arivell who lets the dark things brood large in her head.'

'So what are you going to do?'

'Summon Moshto, the god of life, and ask him to tell his three sons to drive the shadows from her mind.'

'And how are you going to manage to do that?'

'I don't know!' I truth-told Mary. 'I only know that the answer has something to do with gold.'

'If our gods work the same way as yours, good versus evil and all that,' Mary said thoughtfully, 'why don't we call on the powers of them both?'

I nodded as I dragged the potatoes from the fire, being very careful not to burn my fingers. 'Good idea, if we can just work out how!'

I hollowed a hook in the end of a wooden stick with my knife, and poked holes into the half-cooked spuds, pulling out a core of half-cooked potato white, which I mashed down on a plate.

'Pass the jam please, Mary.'

'Jam! In potatoes?'

'You wait until you see how it tastes!'

Mary passed the strawberry jam. I mixed it with the pulp and stuffed back as much as I could into the jackets, using the blunt end of my wooden tool. When I had done, I put them back into the fire to finish baking.

'If your gods and mine are to work together,' Mary said, 'I know a special place, somewhere where good things might happen.'

'Where?'

'The little church, the one at the bottom of your garden.'

'It looks a normal enough place to me,' I told Mary.

'Well, it's not! As your great-gran would say, looks are not everything.'

It was my turn to finish a chain, but mine was made of bright yellow buttercups. It had taken longer to make because the stems are more difficult to hole, and anyway, I had been chitty-chatter-tongued. I copied Mary, and put my chain round Penny's neck. She was beginning to look really pretty. I had never seen her look so good before.

'Once, a long time ago, the church was cursed by a wicked witch.'

'There's no such things as witches, only wise women,' I teased.

'Witches can be black or white, gods can be good or evil, magic can heal or destroy, Freya! At the moment your magic is downright rubbish, so just for once in your life, *listen!*'

I stopped being a rattle-pot. She was right.

'In olden times, if witches were found, they were burned at the stake.'

I nodded, remembering how my great-gran had told me that before.

'One witch who was burned,' Mary continued, 'cursed the church at the bottom of Aunt Emma and Uncle Jack's garden.'

'But it's not *that* old.'

'No, but it's built on the site of a really ancient church. If you go inside, you can still see signs of the really old bits.

'Where?'

'By the altar mainly. You *must* have been in there with Aunt Emma.'

I nodded. 'Yes, but I didn't pay much heed, I'm really not an inside-church person.'

'You should be as nosy as you usually are, then you'll find there's much more to churches than stone,' Mary told me firmly.

'Why did the witch curse the church?'

'Wouldn't you, if the village folk dragged you from it kicking and screaming? She claimed she wasn't a witch, and had simply gone there to pray. The villagers would have none of it. There had been a black cat right by the side of her, all through the service. As she got up to leave, the cat disappeared.'

'I expect the pew caught the sun, cats like that.'

'There had never before been a ghostly cat in the church, witches were far more common. In those days anyone who was strange, risked being called a witch. The woman swore blind that she had never once seen the cat, that it was nothing to do with her, but still they dragged her away.'

Mary's story was scary, so scary that I forgot to

be surprised when Penny took my hand. I held it tight, but never took my eyes off Mary.

'So what did she do then?'

'She pointed her long-fingernailed hand and made a curse,' Mary said, throwing her arms out dramatically, in the hope that I would be so interested I would keep my mouth buttoned up tight and not spoil her story.

'The witch-woman said that any priest who stayed in the parish would be ill or nearly dead before his second Christmas there.'

'And?' It was my turn to be head-on-knee listening.

'From then on, that's how it was. Priests came, and they died, until everyone believed. After that the church's bishop decreed that the clergy need only stay one year.'

I nudged the fire with my toe, and added another of Penny's big logs. 'Go on!'

'Each priest only stayed a year, right up to when a Reverend Adams came. He was a stubborn man. He told the bishops that he was going to put his trust in God . . . and stay. One day, on exactly the anniversary of the day that the cursing witch had died, a small baby boy was found abandoned on the steps of the church. Nobody would help him because they thought that he must have once belonged to the witch. They shook with fear and left him to starve.'

I glanced at Penny, worried whether a baby story would make her cry. She was wide-eyed and interested but, apart from that, just Penny.

'They tried to find a witch to keep him, each to his own, so to speak, but nobody was going to admit to being a witch, even if they wanted a baby very much. Witches, after all, were sooner or later burned at the stake.'

'So they left him?'

'Yes, they left him to die, but in the end Reverend Adams rescued the baby. Some say that he decided that, as he was getting sick anyway, and was almost certain to die of the curse before too long, he might as well raise the child for as long as he could. Others are adamant that he was quite sure from the start that he could conquer the curse for ever.'

I was silent-spellbound, even when I tested the potato-sweets. They were soft and fully cooked. I wrapped them in wads of tissues and handed them to Mary and Penny. Nobody ate anything. We were far too busy listening to Mary, and anyway the potato-sweets were far too hot.

'Reverend Adams lectured the parish from the old altar. He said that the power of God was greater than the power of the witch, and God had decided to prove it once and for all by saving his life and that of the witch-child.'

'And was he right?'

'Of course he was! His sickness vanished, the baby grew up big and strong, and – this is the odd bit – the boy was ordained a holy man too.'

'If that was ages ago, why is the church still special now?'

'Because nothing has changed.' Mary gave me a triumphant smile. 'Every priest in that church was once an abandoned baby, specially left so he can grow up to serve his people. Even your Reverend Plumpton was found on the cold stone steps, but old Ma Plumpton never likes anyone to talk of *that*. She thinks rejected babies are not nice to mention.'

'Or are heathen-spooky.'

'Well, certainly it's not normal to have *so many* just left!'

For a while nobody spoke. We were all thinking about the story, and stuffing ourselves puff-mouth full with hand-hot potato-sweet. We munched them happily, even Penny, who looked like a princess wearing our butter and daisy flowers. They shone in the sun like glitter jewels. They put a flash of an idea in my head, but before I could grab it, it was gone. I racked my brains but was left only with the feeling something had escaped me.

I gave up and turned the remaining potato-sweets. 'You're right! They're very moreish,' Mary admitted, helping herself to yet another.

'Mary,' I said, sucking mine down to its very black skin. 'If Moshto sends me some magic, do you think we could use your special church to help to get it to work?'

'How?'

'I don't know, yet. I just feel that that is the place. After all, it's got its own sort of baby-chain, hasn't it?' I mouth-chewed a really tough bit of skin while I thought. 'Only thing is, I don't really fancy asking the Reverend Plumpton to help, do you?'

10 Uncle Norman

My great-gran says there is a time and a place for everything. It rained for days so neither Mary's gods nor mine could have been in the mood for magic. We made the best of being all-indoor stuck, and played games.

'Mary, don't even breathe!'

'I'll huff and I'll puff and . . .'

'*Mary*!' I removed my hand carefully and glared at my closest friend. Mary just leaned back in her chair and laughed.

We were building a tower of straws on the kitchen table. We had to add the straws one by one, making sure that none of the others moved. Every time someone laid a straw the others planned a forfeit. Penny still wouldn't mouth-speak, so she just had to do as she was told.

'If it falls, or any of the straws move, then you have to wash up,' Mary reminded me. It didn't, even though she was gusting her words out to try.

The tower was right up over our heads. It had taken ages to grow that high. It was a good game but, by now, I longed to go outside with Maggie. The walls of the house were beginning to feel as tight as a drumskin.

Mary picked up a straw.

'If it moves, you have to get up three mornings in a row and greet the sunrise, on your hands and knees, that is. We'll be there too, just to make sure you know what a sunrise is!'

Did Penny smirk? Did I really eye-spot that? Was it worth playing on after all?

'Yeah! Fat chance!' Mary muttered, carefully placing her straw on the very top of the pile.

'Yeah! Fat chance!' Uncle Jack echoed, winking at Uncle Norman, who had just come into the room and was standing behind Penny.

'It's my turn to tell Penny's forfeit,' I told Mary. At the same time I gave her a little shrug, one that meant, look over your shoulder quietly and see who's between you and Penny.

Mary took a sneaky glance, and gave me a knowing wink. Penny was still totally absorbed in the game.

'Penny, if the tower collapses, then you have to

lift your skirt and show Uncle Norman your knickers.'

Penny's face went fresh-sheet white. She leaped from the table, sending our tower into the air like flying spaghetti.

If I had hoped that she would squeal, 'Oh no! Not Uncle Norman!' I was very, very wrong indeed.

Penny shot out of the door before we could collapse into great big giggle-heaps, poor Pudding Pot Penny had no laughing lips at all!

'That was cruel, Freya!' Uncle Jack shouted so loud that my ears hurt, and my laughing stopped in the middle, and left me splutter-full coughing.

'Sorry,' Mary said, as I couldn't. 'We wouldn't really have made her show Uncle Norman her knickers.'

I couldn't help it, I started laughing again. Even just imagining Penny showing Uncle Norman her underwear was too silly for words.

'Freya, you knew Penny would leap up at the very mention of my name,' Uncle Norman said quietly. 'Did you have to do that, when you *know* I'm trying so hard to show her I'm a friend?'

'I only wanted to see her knock the tower over,' I fibbed, wishing I was free in the summer-toss winds like Maggie. 'The game was getting numb-bum boring anyway.'

'You were cruel,' Uncle Jack told me firmly. 'So, as a punishment, you will be doing the washing-up all week.'

Mary sat as quiet as a church mouse. She is not one for washing-up, is Mary.

'Why *did* Penny jump so high?' I asked innocently, as I piled some cups into the sink.

'You *know* why, Freya.'

'No, I don't.'

'Of course you do.' Uncle Jack's tone was softer now. 'Penny's traumatised, she's all shocked and mixed up. Her mum was in a hurry and wouldn't listen, so Penny is full of anger and pain and everyone here has to suffer. On top of that she wants her mother punished, she wants Norman punished, but, most of all, she has punished herself.'

'She doesn't really hate *you*, Uncle Jack, or Aunt Emma, just Uncle Norman.' I knew I was trouble-causing, I couldn't help it. I was poky-long-nose curious about why Penny hated nice Uncle Norman. He was only Jack's pop-in-and-out brother after all.

Uncle Norman gave Mary and me a funny

smile. 'She has to let off steam somehow. She has to show her hate to somebody.'

'And she's picked you?'

Uncle Norman nodded. 'I suppose I should be *honoured* that she has chosen to hate *me* so much.' He didn't look honoured, his face was tumble-troubled, his eyes dressed-touchy tense.

I had to ask why. I felt that something important was just out of reach, something just too close to see. I opened my mouth but Uncle Jack nudged me firmly. He wasn't having his best brother wound up any more. I gave up.

Uncle Norman fixed his face with a smile, patted my shoulder, and put on a teasing voice that was just a *mite* scratchy.

'Why, Freya! Sprite of the woodlands, I really think I've got you this time. Surely you recognise the problem, you with the pure Romany blood in your veins . . .'

'Know what?' I asked, well aware that Mary was so fascinated that she didn't dare break into words in case she risked spoiling things. 'What don't I know?'

We stared up at him, wearing huge question-mark eyes. The room was drop-pin quiet, so quiet that our heartbeats felt like throbbing drums. I knew we looked every bit like hungry puppies. Uncle Jack spluttered, loosened his fingers and tried to cover his amusement. Uncle Norman caught his mood, he laughed, and his voice was almost as deep and musical as Uncle Jack's.

'Freya, now is not the moment, but I'll give you a clue. Nothing is achieved without effort, both love and hate need feeding as they are only a kiss apart. It is *indifference* that is the real destroyer. Surely your wonderful great-grandmother taught you that!'

11 Mary's House

Penny had stayed glue-stuck close to me and Magpie ever since I'd bathed her eyes in dew-kissed gold. Things at least have improved, but she still can't bear to look at the baby Briar Rose, not even when she is full of chuckle-face baby giggles.

Penny Pudding Brain isn't the only one suffering. Sometimes I feel split in two. I want Penny to get better, but I'd love to go walking, just once, pushing the pram holding baby Rose. I have this itchy idea that babies are beginning to grow on *me*.

I feel grumble-grouse cross, too, that Aunt Emma and Uncle Jack are not having things easy. They pussyfoot about, keeping their precious baby as far away from Penny Bootle as possible. If she is near, they try not to tease or play too much. It's not right. It makes life hard for me as well. They give me the eye talk that means, can't you take Penny out for a while? We can't always be outside, especially as Penny doesn't *really* play.

I have to make Penny understand that Rose and Katya are not nearly the same. She has to learn not to hate every baby that breathes, just because they make hurting waves in her shock-damaged head.

With all this going on, it wasn't hard to persuade Aunt Emma and Uncle Jack that it might be a good idea if we went to Mary's house for a couple of days. They were even happy to let us go by bus. Patient Aunt Emma was becoming fractious-full. She, with the soft butter-gold heart, was more than a bit willing to see us gone.

'Now you can spoil my Briar,' I whispered to Aunt Emma as Mary and Penny headed off down the drive, 'but remember, not *too* much!'

'Would I?' Aunt Emma teased, already looking more easy-minded than she had for ages. 'Would *I* do that?'

I laughed as I raced to catch up with the others. I knew full-heart well that she would.

'I'm not sorry to be going home,' Mary admitted as I paid our fares.

'Me neither.'

Mary grinned. 'Pity she has to come too,' she mimed as Penny stared vaguely out of the grubby window.

'You will come back with us though? You will help till the very end?'

'If I must, if you *really* need me.'

'Oh, Mary,' I said taking her hand, 'I do need your help to work this magic.' I opened the carry bag so that Maggie could poky-nose pry as we travelled.

'It's so quiet at Aunt Emma's. The atmosphere is really strange, everyone trying to keep that poor baby quiet.'

'When we get to Mary's, Penny,' I said, turning to my silent shadow, 'you'll have to put up with James. He's growing towards two so he's not really a baby.'

'He *is* still a baby.'

'He's only a baby, Mary, because you gorgios mollycoddle so. Back home, your James would be learning to help. He would be shown herbs to pick, and wood to gather. He'd even be taught how to smile and offer heather to passing gorgios.'

'Like a slave?'

'No, of course not! Like a valuable family member, who's big enough to help in a small but important way. Who could resist the winning smile of an angelic young boy? And, anyway, he'd think it was fun.'

'Well, I think that nearly two is too small.'

'Well, of course you do, you's a gorgio.' I gave my friend a big smile to show her I was teasing. 'No sign of baby number eight then?'

Mary shuddered. 'I was so embarrassed the last time. Oh, Freya, I hope she doesn't get pregnant again. All my school-friends reckon she's better than rabbits at making babies.'

I laughed. Aunt Sally had more babies than any of us Romanies. She would have been like the old woman who lived in a shoe, except that she was still very pretty, and her house was even bigger than Aunt Emma's.

'I'd die,' Mary continued, 'if she had another. Everybody else's mother has stopped having babies years ago, everybody's except mine.'

'Yes, she's certainly been busy-bee broody. Will you have millions too?'

'Not likely,' Mary giggled. 'Will you?'

I shrugged. 'My mam says I might, but I think that the bubbo Briar Rose is quite enough for me.'

It was Mary's dad, Uncle Desmond, who met us off the bus. 'Why hello, girls . . . and you must be Penny, how very nice to meet you.'

Mary grimaced. I knew that she was wondering

how her father would feel, after knowing Penny for two whole days.

'I see you've brought that smelly magpie.'

'She comes everywhere. She's only in the carry bag so as not to upset the bus conductor.'

'Is it house-trained yet?'

'Why should it be? When I'm home she's feather-spread free.'

'And I suppose at our house it's different.'

I nodded. The Reed house was huge. Maggie-Magpie needed to know that I was close, though now she is bigger, I expect she'll want to stay mostly outdoors.

'Bedroom and playroom only then,' Uncle Desmond said, 'and you clear up.'

I nodded. 'I promise. Aunt Emma and Uncle Jack have tickle-telled me all about elbow grease.'

Uncle Desmond gave me a huge hug. 'Oh good!' He was happy, now that the rules were set. He even stroked Magpie.

'Uncle Desmond?'

'Yes, Freya,' Uncle Desmond said, using the tone grown-ups choose when they know they are going to be asked a favour.

'Could Penny and I do some painting? Mary

too, if she wants. Could we paint on the playroom wall?'

The Reed family playroom is in the attic. It runs right round the top of the house. Uncle Desmond is a graphic designer, and he's brilliant at painting anything and everything. The playroom walls are all hand-painted. Lions, tigers, princesses, dragons, rabbits and bears. It's a wonderful place.

'Can you paint?'

'Well, you showed me.'

'So I did!' Uncle Desmond grinned, pleased that I had remembered. 'I'd quite forgotten.'

I knew he was teasing. Uncle Desmond never forgot anything, nothing at all. His brain was big-owl wise and his habits picky-perfect.

'Can we paint tomorrow?'

'Tomorrow!'

'*Please!*'

'Freya, I will go and whitewash the south-facing wall tonight, just for you. It's time we had a change anyway. It will be dry enough for you to decorate by the morning.'

'Thanks, Uncle Des.' I gave him a big sloppy gorgio kiss. 'Thank you ever so much!'

'And, Freya.'

'Yes, Uncle Des?'

'The paintings had better be good!'

By now, Aunt Sally had rushed out of the house to hug us all. Penny wasn't best pleased. She stood like a cold concrete pillar, but she had to put up with being cuddled too. Once the hugging was over we raced upstairs to sort out our things. Penny and I were to share Mary's room, which was even larger than our room at Aunt Emma's. In no time at all we were settled and it was time for tea.

We escaped in the evening, Mary and I. We were just a bit cruel. We just couldn't be ever-saints, we'd had more than enough of Pudding Pot Penny. We didn't do anything really bad, we just fell in with Mary's sisters' plans.

Elizabeth and Antonia decided that they could make Penny talk where Mary and I had failed. All they had to do, they decided, was plague Penny with kindness. Within an hour or so Penny Bootle would emerge from her dark secret world butterfly-perfect, and a normal girl again.

Mary and I knew better, but we didn't let on.

'We'll show her some fun.'

'We'll read stories, play in the attic, dress up.'

'We'll have her chatting in no time at all.'

'Easy-peasy.'

Mary and I smiled sweetly as we left the reluctant Penny in their care. I prised her hand from mine, and handed her over to Antonia, who was by far the bossiest sister. 'I'll come back soon, Penny. Now be very good for Toni. You'll enjoy playing with Mary's sisters for a while. I'm sure you will.'

Penny's brooding eyes filled with tears. I ignored them. Mary took my hand, and pulled me away as fast as she dared, just in case I should cry clucky-chicken and change my mind.

'Race you outside,' she said, adding, 'to the tree house,' when the others were out of hearing.

I raced after Mary. Maggie-Magpie flew up over our heads, so she could better keep her beady eye on us. Mary and I fought over who should be first to get to the rickety wooden playhouse hidden in the heart of the great white maple. Mary won. I was more agile, but she knew her way through the branches better.

We sat ourselves down on the plain wooded floor and let our breathing ease. Once you were right in the centre, woolly-wrapped by thick green walls, you were quite safe from the most pryingest eyes in the world.

'Let's face it,' Mary said, 'Penny's never going to talk again.'

'She'll hate it with your sisters. They're not used

to her. They'll nag her wicked when they realise that she's just going to sit around like a stodgy pudding. They'll all get bother-head bored.' I felt guilty. I had made the joining magic with Penny. I shouldn't have left her behind. 'What if they just up and leave her? What then?'

'She's got to learn, even if she's not going to talk, she'll have to fit in with the real world somehow. Sometimes you have to be cruel to be kind.'

I remembered how my dad had once cut the throat of a screaming road-smashed dog, in order to end his suffering quicker. Was leaving Penny like that?

For a while, we just enjoyed being us. We chatted, and Maggie-Magpie squawked. She did more squawking than we did chatting. She was trying to prove to the world that she now owned the tree. Eventually even Maggie fell silent. She sat and preened each feather shimmer-shiny, and when that was properly done, she tucked her head under her wing and went to sleep.

Mary and I ran out of gossipy girl things, and debated what to do next.

'We could follow the garden stream, away up the hill a bit.'

'Mum will go mad if we go off this late.'

'No one will see us.'

'*Someone* will. If I'm punished by not being allowed to come back, how will you do your magic?'

'We could play cat's cradle,' I suggested, desperate for Mary's continued help.

'No string.'

'I wonder how Penny's doing?'

'We could go and find out, check on the others secretly. Now *that* would be fun.'

'How?'

'Follow me.'

We sneaked around the orchard boundary, hedge-hopping, and keeping in the shadows, so as not to be seen.

'I bet they gave up reading in the study ages ago. By now, they're probably in the playroom,' Mary muttered.

'We'll never be able to spy on them up there.'

'Why not?'

'It's far too high, silly.'

'Well, I know how to do it. If we climb that apple tree near the wash-house window, we should be able to get ourselves up on to that flat roof. We can plan our route from there.'

Suddenly Mary was stubborn-faced keen. In no time at all we had shinned down the maple, skirted round the garden, and scrambled up the straggly apple tree, and on to the roof. 'We'll have to scale the sloping roof, the one that leads up from the back of the wash-house roof to the underneath of the bedroom balconies.'

She pointed the way, and I edged up, sitting on the tiles, and bottom squatting a centimetre or two at a time. Mary followed, grinning wildly. We were as quiet as mice, and before too long we had reached the wide ridge at the top of the slope.

Try as I might, I couldn't reach the balcony stone. Twice I lost my balance and nearly slipped. I began to think that I shouldn't have button-lipped my mouth so firmly, the very first moment this silly idea had crept into Mary's head.

Mary was really enjoying herself now. She hadn't done anything so naughty for years. She was taller and that helped. She managed to struggle on to the balcony, and pulled me up beside her.

'Now what?' I asked, hoping that Mary would realise that the next bit was just impossible, and not leave the lip-tremble baby bit to me.

'The playroom is just above the balcony rooms.'

'Can't we climb in here? Can't we tiptoe through the house?'

'We'll be spotted. Mum will be putting James to

bed, or bathing the twins. She could be *anywhere* upstairs.'

'She won't worry,' I said, feeling a bit panicky. Climbing trees was one thing, but scaling giant houses was turning out to be quite another. 'As long as your mother doesn't guess that we window-climbed, she'll be fine.'

'Mum's bound to say hello! Elizabeth has ears like a bat, she'll come and see what's what. I'll bet they can't wait to hand back Penny, and I really must find out if she's driving them mad too.'

'She'll be doing nothing, like she usually does, and anyway does it really matter?'

'Of course it *matters*!'

'This house is so high, Mary, it's *dangerous*.'

Mary ignored me. She was wound up in her adventuring and was not going to stop. She moved slowly away, easing herself up on to a parapet and pointing. 'There's a ledge over there but it's a bit slippery, we'll have to be very careful indeed. It's only a third of the width of that deep pond log.'

I looked at the ledge. All down the side was a straight long drop. There was no sloping roof to break your fall. If we slipped, we would be crash bang splat dead. I was tremble-tight button-lipped now, too frightened to go up or down, and too proud to admit that I was heart-thump scared.

Mary was still hot-head confident. 'There's a fire escape just round the corner, we can creep along until we get there. Once we reach that it's easy.'

'What if we fall?' I stammered, finding my voice at last. 'What will your mother say then? What if . . .?'

'Freya, we won't fall, not if we're careful.'

It was idiot-stupid to try and reach the play-room, but there was no stopping Mary. Suddenly it was *me* gorgio-scared and *her* Romany-wild.

'How will we get back?' I asked, still desperately hoping that she would change her mind.

'Oh, that's easy, we go down the fire escape. Going down, you can check a room is empty before you're spotted. People always look straight ahead, or down over the garden. They never look up.'

I made one last attempt to stop her. 'What if we get killed? Who will work the magic for Penny?'

'Look, chicken, we've done the hard bit. It's not far, just a metre one side of the corner and a metre the other. Surely a little gypsy girl can manage that. I thought you Romanies could do *anything*!'

'So how do we get round the drainpipe?' I was dry-mouth feared, but I had been challenged so I couldn't lose face. If Mary went, then I had to go too.

'We hold the drainpipe . . . don't you know anything about house climbing?'

I shook my head. 'The thing that I usually climb is trees.'

'When you reach the drainpipe,' Mary warned me, 'be careful not to hang on it. It's only fixed with little brackets so just use it for support. Lean against the wall keeping your weight on your feet and your back.'

I nodded. I couldn't think what else to do. I felt all shivered, but there was no stopping Mary when she had quite made up her mind.

I watched, my stomach churning full-cow busy, as Mary crept along the narrow stone facing. After what seemed like hours she reached the downpipe, and clung to it. She was smiling, but she didn't seem all that bright-faced confident to me. Carefully she swung over the pipe and on to the ledge on the other side, then she released her left hand, turned her feet round, oh so carefully, pausing until she felt stable enough to let go with her right hand and steady herself with her left.

I watched, and my stomach was seasick-gluggy by the time Mary had turned the corner, her back rigid against the wall, and disappeared from sight. I watched every movement, every second. I must have stood rooted to the spot for the eternity it took her to reach the safety of the ladder, lean over, and peer into the east window.

'They're on the other side, about to play the old piano. Antonia's just opened the lid, I think they're going to try a singalong.'

'Now you *know*, could you come back this way?'

'Don't be silly, Freya. I never had you marked as a *coward*. Now come along while the music, if that's what it is, is loud enough to drown your whingeing.'

I wished that I had never heard of Mary or Penny. I wished that I had stayed with my mam and great-gran. I wished I was anywhere but here.

'Come on!'

I had no choice. I was Romany-proud. If I chickened out then Mary would tell the others how I was baby-scared. I gritted my teeth and prepared to follow. My back was glued to the wall in terror. My feet moved because my very life depended on it. Mary called out instructions and I obeyed, glad that the stuff that Antonia called music really could drown out the fear in my voice.

I edged along, my fingers blue from gripping as I

tried hard not to remember how far below the nice safe ground was. Just as I felt my head go muzzy and my legs go wobbly, Mary reached out and grasped my hand.

'There! I told you it was easy.'

'I never want to do that again, even if it was easy.'

'Sure thing!' Mary told me cheerfully. 'It was really stupid, but we did it. You only have to do a silly thing once. Everybody does something really silly once. Frances taught us all *that*.'

We peered in through the east-facing window. Antonia was just slamming down the piano lid.

'Well, she obviously doesn't want to sing!'

'And she doesn't want to skip.'

'And she still won't talk.'

'Perhaps she's stupid,' Elizabeth said. 'What if we start her at the beginning?'

Elizabeth and Antonia, very slowly, walked Penny round the great playroom, pointing at paintings and holding her tight to make sure she paid attention.

'Bunny, say *bunny*, Penny.'

'Princess, say *princess*, Penny.'

'Wizard, say *wizard*, Penny.'

Penny Bootle did no such thing. She looked

straight ahead, her eyes dark and unseeing and, just for once, we didn't blame her. Penny was many things, but she wasn't stupid. Both Mary and I had grown confident-sure of that.

After a while they gave up on the word game. Elizabeth quite lost patience. She grabbed Penny by the shoulders and shook her hard.

'Say *Penny*, Penny, or I'll smash your pouty face in.'

I went to climb in through the window but Mary stopped me. 'She won't hit her, silly, not when she can't defend herself properly. She won't hurt Penny any more than you and I would have let her drown.'

Mary was right; Elizabeth raised her fists and threatened, but she didn't strike. Penny either knew that she wouldn't or didn't care. She didn't even blink. Elizabeth gave up. 'Oh come on, stupid, Freya and Mary will be back soon. Come and see the wizards and witches on the wall.'

'Well, so much for easy-peasy,' I said, and Mary giggled.

Satisfied that no miracle had occurred, we climbed down the steel fire-escape steps in no time at all, pausing only to check that each room was empty before we passed to a lower floor. Once, we saw Mary's mother walking about but, as Mary said, she looked out but not up. We reached the ground with no trouble at all.

Maggie-Magpie flew to join us as we neared the door. She had no intention of spending the night outside all alone in a tree, none whatsoever. Safe now, we sauntered inside and went noisily upstairs to see the others.

'Penny talking yet?'

'Nearly,' Antonia lied.

'What? Let me guess. Bunny, princess and wizard, really useful words like that.'

'Are you psychic, little gypsy witch?' Elizabeth asked, her mouth fair spitting venom.

'Of course I am!' Gorgios can *never* outlie a gypsy. We learned hundreds of years ago to live off our wits, it's a deep blood instinct.

They made to come at me . . . both of them menacing. I stood still, and offered my sweetest smile. 'I shouldn't touch me, not if you have an ounce of sense.'

'Why not?' Suddenly they seemed hesitant, not understanding why I hadn't put up my hands or run away.

Mary gave them the answer that was all ready in my head. 'I shouldn't touch her, sisters dear. After all, the thing you'll get back is a cruel gypsy curse.'

They pushed Penny towards me and I took her hand, oddly pleased to feel the warmth of her fingers in mine. 'I'm glad that's sorted,' I told them, ice-mouth pleasant.

The only Reed girl I really like is Mary. She isn't rich-house posh-stuffy, like the others. If they'd have hurt a hair on Penny's head, I'd have made Mary's church witch seem like a holy-halo saint. I might not like Penny very much, but I'm like my great-gran: I never give up and her future depends on *me*.

12 Wall Painting

'I'm going to paint this wall!' I told Penny the following morning, not letting on that Aunt Emma once said Penny used to be a much better painter than me.

Penny carried on doing what she did really well: absolutely nothing.

'I'm going to make a *mural*.' I was full-heart proud of that word. 'Mural,' I said again, just in case Penny had been playing cloth-eared dumb. 'I'm going to make a wall painting that is all about me.'

My best friend Mary raised her eyes to heaven. 'Well, count me out, Freya Boswell. I'm not going to spend all day watching you fool around with paints. I'm going out with my darling sisters. *Anything*'s better than watching you paint.'

'But not much!' I said, using Mary's voice-talk.

Mary glared at me, and I guessed it was because I was close to the truth. Even Mary usually got fed up with her snooty sisters. I offered Mary a smug smile, but she wasn't going to let me off that easy. She turned her attention to Penny. 'Well, Penny, do you want to spend the day drowning in paint, or would you prefer to come out and have some fun?'

Penny never even glanced at Mary. She just stayed tight in my shadow. Those Reed girls had scared her wicked.

'Well, I'm going to mural-paint. Penny can do as she chooses,' I said, pretending not to care. I climbed the stairs to the playroom without even glancing behind me. Penny followed, just as I knew she would.

Uncle Desmond had kept his promise to paint the wall clean white. It was itching to be drawn on, crinkly white hopeful it was. I sat myself down on the floor, and stared at the big white space that screamed *paint me!*

Maggie hopped round on my shoulder and pecked my ears. She wanted to play. I opened the top window to give us some cool air. 'Why don't you do something different?' I whispered to her as I scratched her black feather-head. 'Why don't you practise being a spread-wing bird? Go out and play, find Mary and the girls. Go and annoy them . . . please.'

To my surprise, Maggie hopped straight on to the windowsill, gave me a look that meant I won't be long, and flew away. My mouth was open-gaped as I watched her fly low over the garden, as if she really was looking for Mary. I felt just a tiny bit worried, I *would* be tearful-sad if she went away for ever but I shrugged whisper-breath casual, and settled myself to the task in hand.

Penny sat herself down by my side, her shoulders rubbing mine. I never asked her if she wanted to paint too.

'This is our favourite place,' I told Penny, beginning to outline an ancient hedge with two background oaks. 'I was born here. This place is special to us. We come back here every Easter. Did I tell you I was a Chime Child? We are only born now and then.'

I coloured in fresh springtime grass. I even put in bits of primrose and celandine, growing right on the edge of the trickly stream. It didn't matter if it was a tiny bit smudgy. It was all there . . . perfect . . . in my head.

'A Chime Child is born on Good Friday just as the clock strikes twelve. If you're a Romany too, then this gives you special powers to do things.'

Penny seemed totally unimpressed. I shrugged

and picked up my paintbrush again. I was glad Mary had chosen not to stay. In my head I could hear her saying, *Powers? What powers? Well, painting in a hurry definitely isn't one of them!*

I drew Great-gran's magnificent vardo, being careful to make the wood shiny brown, and the curtains sunshine yellow. It wasn't quite fault free, but the magic was there.

'Like all proper Romanies, I was born in a special birthing tent. My dad put it up between the vardo and the great oak. Inside is always fresh-strewn straw smelling proper good. Romnichals don't get involved, birth is a woman's thing, so there are no men fiddle-fussing, just mams and aunts and grans. The tent is burned up a few weeks after, rather like my great-gran's vardo will be burned when she dies.

'I think the vardo is too special to burn. I think I should have it. It would keep my magic strong, be a link through her to me. That vardo is living history, every memory I have of my great-gran is tied in there somewhere.' I looked at Penny. She stared at me blankly. I don't suppose she'll ever understand how much that vardo means to me, not even when she's full-head sensible.

In my fresh spring field I painted a dark-haired

baby sitting all bright-eye innocent among the sun-kissed flowers. By her side I drew a comfy lady, with rich brown curls and a bright-lined headscarf. 'That's my mam, Penny, that's what she looked like when I was a yearling and a bit. See those great gold earrings? They're proper sovereigns. My dad gave them to her when they were kiss-kiss courting. That pile of green stuff by my mam is herbs. She's binding them up now they're dry. My mam has taught me a lot about herbs . . . but not as much as my great-gran.'

I stopped talking and looked at my mural. So far it looked really good. I felt tipple-tummy trembly as I drew in a strong man with a wicked smile. 'That's my dad!' was all I could manage. Penny sensed my sadness. Deliberately, her hand brushed mine. I held it tight for comfort and, when I turned, I could see she was looking at my life painting real proper. She was actually seeing it.

'My dad went fishing,' I said, after a while. 'We were hungry. The weather was swirl-temper bad. My dad went down to where the river passes the great house estate. There's usually good fishing there, even if it isn't allowed. He took the dogs, all of them – Sabre, Fusty and Woodpile. Sabre is my favourite, but dad's favourite was Woodpile. Woodpile was young then and mighty good at catching rabbits.'

Penny was *listening*. She was looking and listening like any normal girl.

I drew Woodpile with his great loppy legs. They weren't quite right, but they were passing good.

'Vashti, Tashar and my other brothers had gone off deer-hunting before. It wasn't here.' I left a white hazy space to show we were now looking at another place, and then a wider blue-green river, so Penny could see it was deep and dangerous. My body shook with locked-up tears. I drew my lovely dad, lying all body-white, with blood leaking where he had smashed his head on a stone.

'He never came back!' I told Penny, trying to make my voice calm and not bitter-sad. 'While he was fish-tickling he slipped, bashed his head on a rock, and fell into the water. Sabre, Fusty and Woodpile tried real hard to drag him out of the water, they even left teeth marks deep in his arms and down his back.'

I wiped away escaping tears with a green-smeared hand. Penny's eyes stared at me, big and brown and living-looking. She hung tightly on to my hand.

'They tried real hard, them dogs. When they got

116

him out they cuddled up real tight to try and keep him warm . . . all except Woodpile, who went to find my brothers.' I sniffed back my sadness, and tried to look gypsy-strong. 'My dad was dead before my brothers found him.'

I drew a fancy cart carrying my dad's coffin. I painted in the red berries and dark green leaves that we had gathered to make it look I-love-you good. I drew my mam and my brothers, all trying hard not to look sad.

'Later, after the service, we had to sing, dance and play music, to send him home. We started slowly to show him we would miss him, that we wished he could stay. Then we realised that goodbye is not for ever and we wanted the best for him. He could only have that if he went on to the happy place. Vashti offered his heart to his violin. Penny, you have never ever heard such strange and won-derful music. The dancing too became louder and louder, wilder and wilder, stranger and stranger. That way Dad knew that he must pass on, that he had to leave, and we wouldn't waste time grieving for him.

'All his things were burned while we played that loud music, everything that was his . . . except the metal wagon that he insisted stay for my mam, and

117

a few memento things. My dad thought only clothes and linen should be burned. He said breaking china and burning wagons was wasteful. I wish he could get that idea into the head of my ostrich great-gran!

'A vardo is a proper Romany caravan. Ours has big wooden wheels and is painted in lift-heart bright colours. I wish you could see that vardo, Penny. I'm sure you'd love it nearly as much as me.

'Anyway, like I said, we don't shed many tears. We try to sing and dance. My mam says it's no good crying if you believe in a happy place. She says you have to follow your own pathway, so it's best to be strong and get on with things. She says every tear shed is a precious wasted moment.'

I sighed, and gave Penny a hug. 'My mam hid her heartsick and got on with living, but even my mam cried, alone in the blackness of night, when she thought we was sandman-sleeping. My mam is very special.' I stared at my painting, trying to be as Romany-certain as my mam.

Slowly, I became aware that Penny had picked up a paintbrush. She was quietly inspecting the little pots of paint. I dared not move a muscle. I carried on with my life-tells as if nothing at all had happened.

'When my sister was born my mam had a new

birthing tent. This time, Tashar, my brother, made it for her when she was near her due time. I was allowed in the tent because I was a girl. I was quite big then . . . about five summers, I think.

'I saw Pansy born. She was my first sister, after all them brothers. She was born all blue. At first my mam was not too concerned, babies are often born that way, but when my cousin, Lurenda, smacked little Pansy to make her lungs breathe in the fresh cool air, she stayed blue, she never turned healthy pink.

'Lurenda called out a gorgio doctor. I knew then that Moshto's third son had laid his hands on our baby Pansy. The doctor came and shook his head. He never even tried to take her away. He knew it would make no difference to the time of Pansy's dying.

'We spent three precious days with my baby sister. My mam only ever got her to take tiny suck-sips of milk. I gave her a little bath soon after she was birthed. Lurenda let me hold her all by myself. I was real careful not to let her get cold, but she still stayed break-heart blue.

'We loved her properly much, Penny, even though she wasn't perfect-made. She was a tiny scrap of only just living, but she was still my only sister.

'She's so brave, my mam. First she lost my dad, and then my sister. She never shed no tumble-tears in front of my brothers, nor in front of me, but I've seen her pillow stained weeping-wet in the morning. Oh yes, I have.'

Penny said nothing. She stood by my side. In one hand she clutched a paintbrush, with the other she reached for a palette of paint.

I still never let on that I noticed. I drew my dad, all head-better. I drew him holding our baby Pansy, but this time she was new-life pink. I drew them sunshine-happy. 'My mam is sure that they are both in a happy place. She says we'll meet again . . . and that is why it wouldn't hurt my great-gran to leave me her vardo. She says Great-gran and Pansy, and so that must mean Katya too, are bound to go to that happy place. *Everyone* who is deep-heart kind goes there.'

Penny was painting now, and I had to admit she was far far better at painting than me. Her strokes were swift and firm, her picture much more alive than she had ever been so far.

Penny drew a railway line and a fast approaching train. She drew it so well that I could hear the

warning horn and smell her fear. She drew it
dragon-strong and giant-scary. Right above it she
painted in her baby sister, Katya . . . blowing like a
tiny pink tissue in the wind.

I sucked in fright-shocked air, somehow I could
see Katya disappearing. One moment there, one
moment gone.

In the desperate silence that followed we clung
together, crying great salty tears. We were joined.
Two as one. We were crying for Katya and Pansy,
and for Penny and me.

When, at last, we were wrung out with being
sob-filled, when we had both begun to feel the quiet
healing of salty tears, I dragged Penny back to the
wall.

'Paint Katya, Penny! Paint her with my dad and
Pansy. Put her in the happy-place picture, Penny,
go on! Put her safely there in the picture, so you can
start to live for yourself again.'

Penny and I stared at each other, both our faces
well and truly smudged with painty tears. I grasped
her shoulders and stared deep into her sad brown
eyes. 'It's really important, Penny. You have to
have the courage to set her free.'

It seemed like for half of for ever that Penny
and me stood eye to eye, will to will. In my head I

summoned the power of the joining magic. I tightened my grip on her shaking shoulders, trying to send the importance of the doing deep into her mind.

'*Paint Katya, Penny. You must put her in a happy place.*'

For endless ages nothing happened. Then, very slowly, Penny picked up the paints. She drew Katya, sweet-faced and smiling. She drew her held safe in the arms of my dad, held close to my baby sister Pansy.

13 Happy Shoes

Things have improved. Penny is three parts well since our mural-paint. She mostly smiles and she joins in all our games. She's not Pudding Pot Penny any more . . . it's just that her chatter-tongue is still not set free.

Maggie-Magpie came back when I called. I thought that she would. Like me, Maggie-Magpie has no intention of staying at the great white mansion for ever. We're restless things. To us, a posh house is only a cage with frills. Maggie and me belong to woods and fields. Even going back to Aunt Emma's won't ease my homesick heart-strings.

Aunt Emma and Uncle Jack arrived to collect us on time. I feel tumbled-up desperate. I only have two more weeks to find the curing magic, because then Mary has to go back to school. I feel in my bones that she must be with us until Penny's wholly happy.

'I'd supposed she'd be talking by now,' Mary whispered, as we carried our things upstairs.

'Aunt Emma and Uncle Jack say a miracle is likely to take a little time. Uncle Norman told them that she was frightened to set her locked-up anger free. I think he's right, don't you?' I spoke clearly as I wanted Penny to hear. 'Why should she carry on suffering? It wasn't her fault that they crossed the railway line when the lights flashed red that day.'

'Perhaps she thinks she should have seen the train sooner.'

'It was round the bend . . . and even if she had seen it, what on earth was she supposed to do?'

Mary and I both made big shrugs. We were trying to show Penny that we deep-heart cared.

'I wish Penny *would* believe,' I told Mary as Uncle Jack drove us all back, 'especially as we went to so much effort to put Katya into a special place.'

'What?' Mary looked wrinkle-faced puzzled.

I took Penny's hand, and gave it a squeeze. 'Katya is with Pansy.'

'Oh! You mean in heaven?'

I wasn't sure, but to my surprise, Penny nodded.

'So if the babies are happy now, why won't Penny talk?'

'I think that my magic is not quite finished. The telling hour has not quite come.'

'Oh, you and your silly magic, Freya Boswell!'

I shoved Mary, and she shoved me back, to show we were still best friends. After unpacking, we all went down to the kitchen for welcome-home treats.

'I've checked on Briar Rose,' Uncle Jack was saying. 'She's sleeping peacefully, Em. Now if you don't mind, I'll pop into the office. I'm so behind at the moment.'

We share grins, all three of us. Uncle Jack was always far too busy to stay home for long.

'Norman is coming over,' Aunt Emma reminded him, and Penny promptly lost her grin. I wish I understood why she hates Uncle Norman.

'I won't be long,' Uncle Jack said, giving us all kisses, but we didn't believe him. He always said that too.

'How's Penny's mother?' I asked, to see how Penny reacted. To my surprise she turned her eyes towards Aunt Emma, and waited for her to answer.

'Well, as I said, a badly broken body takes a long time to mend.' Aunt Emma paused, and still Penny was watching her face. Aunt Emma took a big breath. 'Frances is very depressed. I think she needs to see *you*, Penny, before she gets really better.'

We sat deathly still, waiting for Penny to shake or scream, but she didn't! She just nodded very slowly, and her saucer eyes filled with tears.

We smiled and hugged her, telling her she was kind. Penny nodded again, but her face was not happy-filled.

'I think Sunday is a good day,' Aunt Emma continued. 'That way you can prepare, make her a little card perhaps, and if I give you some extra pocket-money, it would be nice if you could choose her a little present.'

Penny looked panic-stricken. I guessed that if she could speak, she would tell us she'd changed her mind. I felt that she needed us too. 'What if we all go?' I said quickly. 'And we all choose a card and a present.'

'Good idea!' Aunt Emma said. 'That way, Frances will see how busy you've been, and how well you've got on together.'

Penny still looked face-pasty white. Aunt Emma hugged her close. 'Your mother will understand, Penny. She *knows* that everyone has to recover from shock in their very own way. She doesn't *blame* you for staying away for so long.'

Penny's face was all blood-drained. She looked like she would faint at any moment. 'Can we sleep in the tent tonight?' I asked, desperate to change the subject.

'On our own, no grown-ups,' Mary added, ever ready to back me in taking advantage of a moment.

'And can we cook supper ourselves?' I added. 'It will help Penny to be kept busy till Sunday.'

'What will you cook?' Aunt Emma asked, looking a hint suspicious.

'I could cook hotchi-witchi!' I teased, but Mary remembered what it was.

'We're not having hedgehog!' she told me firmly. 'Hedgehog is *off*.'

'You can have sausages, baked potatoes, and baked beans,' Aunt Emma said. 'If you promise to be very careful indeed.'

We went upstairs to plan, but a funny thing happened. One minute I was sitting on the bed talking to Mary and Penny, the next I was back with my mam. I could feel her clutching my hand, even though I knew I wasn't there.

'You look poorly, Gran,' she was saying. 'I think we should summon our Chime Child. I think Freya should come back home.'

'You're not using *me* as an excuse to fetch her

127

back. No, you'll do no such thing!' Great-gran stormed, but she was looking ghostly-face pale. She must be feeling poorly. Normally she'd have known instantly that I was spirit travelling.

Anyhow, she still stuck her chin out all proud. 'I don't need no Chime Child to tell me how to die, and anyway she has work not finished. She *can't* come home, not till it's properly done.'

'But, Ostrich,' my mam said, 'she'll *want* to be here at your passing. It's not fair that she should be missing. Surely she must be allowed to come?'

Great-gran shook her head. In her ears she wore her favourite sovereigns. They chinked on their gold chains, and seemed almost bigger than she was.

'The Chime Child stays!'

'But she loves you.'

'I want to come home!' I mind-talked as loud as I could. 'I could safely leave Penny for a couple of days. She's *nearly* well.'

Suddenly, Great-gran heard. 'Those days are important days!' Her words rang loud in my ears. 'You have made a link with dew-water and gold. You are bonded, until the magic is over. *You must not break the bond.*'

My eyes filled with tears, gypsy tears that should never be shed. Great-gran was mind-thinking proper now, her wrinkled old face softened. Many miles away I felt the warmth of her smile, and heard the love in her voice. 'Chime Child, you have special gifts. You will know the moment of my crossing. Dear heart, you will be with me. If you were at the other end of this great earth, you would still be clutched to my heart. *Believe*.'

The shutters came down. I was back on my bed with Mary and Penny, who were totally unaware that I had ever been away. I tried to remember the things that I had told Penny so many times. My great-gran wasn't just dying. She was preparing to leave for a happy place. I should be Romany-smiling not wearing a tear-filled gorgio face.

If Mary sensed my sadness she was wise enough to say nothing, and I was grateful for that.

'Let's make this a real adventure!' I said, pushing my sad-thinks aside.

I inspected the neat little sleeping-bags, laid out in a row. It was like being in a tent house, not exciting at all. We live like that quite often.

'If we were on a poaching trip,' I said, thinking of my dad, 'we'd just have a blanket, or these days a bag, and we'd sleep under a hedge looking up at the stars.'

'It would be cold!'

'Not in a bag, and certainly not in summer. That tent will be all sticky-skin hot with three of us. You wait and see.'

'You want us to sleep in the hedge?' Mary said, her voice rising. 'Aunt Emma and Uncle Jack will go mental.'

'Not if they don't find out!'

Penny looked interested! Penny looked really interested. She nudged Mary, who saw it was two to one, and softened.

'I suppose we could sleep in the tent till they checked . . . and then creep out.'

That settled, there was lots to do. Now we had a secret to share, camping was much more fun. During the afternoon we gathered great armfuls of dry wood, from the copse on the edge of Endall Common, being ever so careful to make sure they were dry and good for burning.

Endall Common is not the least bit scary in the daytime. Not like it was at dawn, when Penny and I did the joining magic.

Aunt Emma and Uncle Jack left us to it. I think they slipped out to the hospital with Uncle Norman and Briar Rose. We were told to be good, and if there was trouble to go next door. There wouldn't be trouble, why did they think there might be?

The hardest thing was finding places in the hedge where we could tuck in and sleep at night. One place is easy to find, but three, and close together so you can whisper talk under the stars, is struggle-brain difficult. The best thing to find is hollows ready formed in the ground, like fox and badger runs. We had to break off a few small branches, but not so many that the hedge was damaged. We didn't want Mrs Plumpton next door to get fuss-pot angry.

'Why *are* we sleeping in the hedge?'

'To keep us away from prying eyes, and to keep us dry.'

'It won't rain.'

'Don't argue! Do you want the world to see your secret sleep-ways? Anyway, the hedge will mop up your snores.'

'I *don't* snore.'

'You do.'

'I don't.'

'She does, doesn't she, Penny?' Penny nodded and giggled, but she didn't speak.

Ages it took, to make three people-holes real close . . . absolutely ages. When we had done, we laid out some fresh grass, fetched, like the wood, from Endall Common. The grass would make us comfy, keep us warm, and stop the sleeping-bags from getting tell-tale grubby. We went back and forwards time and time again. It was a good job Endall Common was not too far!

I made a nice safe cooking place, not a bit near to the hedge. I dug up a square of the grass and carefully put it in the shade, even though it was in Aunt Emma's wild bit of garden. I did it so we could leave things real good, just like we did at home. That way, Aunt Emma and Uncle Jack would know we had kept our word about being grown-up care-ful, and the foxes, frogs and rabbits would stay hop-skip happy.

Mary and Penny stacked up our cooking wood, not too near the fire place, and not too near the hedge. They made the stacks neat and tidy, as if they were proper Romanies.

'Why there?'

'Well, the wood won't catch up in the hedge, but it will be given some shelter if it rains.'

'I told you! It won't rain!' Mary said, looking up at a clear blue sky.

'Well, we'll do it anyway,' I muttered. So we did things all careful, and when we cooked, we only added what we needed to give us cooking hotness. My mam would have been real proud. We shared out our cooking. Penny had to watch the baked potatoes, turning them carefully, so they grew black but not burnt. Mary did the same with the sausages, and I looked after the beans.

The beans cooked real quick. Mary said that I chose them because I'm a real bossy-boots, and that way I had plenty of time for giving orders. The trouble with Mary is that she is often right.

Fresh-air meals are lip-smacking good. Mary, Penny and I had worked real hard all day, getting things ready and making plans. By the time we had eaten our meal, it was really quite late and time for bed. It was getting summer-time dark, and just for once we didn't mind a bit.

We lay in our tent like three little angels, until Aunt Emma and Uncle Jack crept in to kiss us goodnight, and then – as soon as it was safe – we crept outside.

It was too dark to move Maggie-Magpie. She was wing-tucked in her carry bag. She only opened one eye as we went. We left her to guard.

Like snug little rabbits we curled up in our people-size holes. The stars were shimmer-twinkle bright, and we could see nearly as clear as day. The branches covered around us, making a nice safe shield. I felt like I was having a home sort of fun. I felt outside-air comfy. I felt closer to home.

My great-gran would be out under these very same stars. She would be lying all peaceful, deciding the time of her passing. We Romanies can do that. We like to die as we are born, full-spirit free. I begged her to wait till I could be with her. I mind-sent her love and kisses; I sent kisses too, to my mam and dibby gran. I was night-time-out happy, but I missed my family. I was even a little scared that Dibby might forget me. She does, after all, forget lots of things.

Suddenly we heard footsteps.

'What's that?'

'Sh!'

The footsteps grew closer. Penny coughed.

'Sh!'

'They're not in the tent!' Aunt Emma's voice rose shrill in the still night air. 'Jack, they're gone! Call the police!'

We kept still, all of us cold-heart scared. I'd never dreamed that they'd call the police. Why, anyone should have guessed that three little girls would not go far, especially when they had left a magpie to guard.

'For God's sake, Jack! Do something!'

We'd be told off good and proper for this. It was far too bad for just cross-patch tongues. Poor Aunt Emma was going frantic.

We all lay quiet, trying to make up our minds what to do . . . all except Penny, who let out another nervous little cough. For a tongue-tied topsy, she was making a lot of tickle-throat noises!

I wasn't sure whether to laugh or cry. I wanted us to be left and yet I almost wished to be found. It wasn't right that they should be deep-heart scared, not when they had always been so kind. I lay all muddle-brained. I hated them fretting, but I didn't want to be the one to spoil our adventure, not when we had worked so very hard all day.

I knew Mary would stay still until the very last moment. Anyone who could plan a roof-top climb would not be the least bit frightened of a little hedge adventure, but me, I was a bit scared. I hate angry mouth-tellings from gorgios, but I was mostly worried about upsetting heart-sick Penny. I didn't want to end this adventure, after all. *Penelope Bootle was really joining in.*

Cough, cough.

Aunt Emma still had her head buried deep in the tent.

Cough, cough, cough.

135

'Jack, all I can see is that stupid magpie! Jack, what are we going to do?'

'Are the sleeping-bags there?'

'No! There's nothing. Just a wide-eyed bird that's cross at being woken.'

Uncle Jack turned towards the sound of Penny's muffled coughs, but his eyes were unseeing. He was just gazing vaguely out into the night like my half-woken bird. 'No sleeping-bags?' he asked Aunt Emma again, his voice almost uninterested.

I started to shiver despite the warm night air. Uncle Jack didn't sound too concerned. Had he seen? Or had we been too naughty this time? Had he decided he didn't care whether we were lost or not, that Pudding Pot Penny, strong-willed Mary and a little wild gypsy were all a bad influence on his precious Briar Rose?

'Get a torch! We'll start searching.'

'Really, Em! It's dark. Wait till morning.'

'But *anything* could have happened. Anything!'

For a moment Uncle Jack was silent, his eyes still somewhere between me and the sound of Penny's muffled cough. I lay as still as I could, hardly daring to breathe. Penny and Mary were masked by the woodpile in front of the hedge, but me, if I even muscle-twitched I could be seen if he looked real careful, but gorgios rarely do. In the end I had to do it. I'd been glue-stuck muddle-headed for far too long. I made a tiny mouse-type rustle.

Mary sensed I was uneasy-minded. 'Keep quiet,' she hissed.

'Jack, I'm not joking! They're gone. We *have* to organise a search.'

'No! I don't think so. It would be better to wait till morning. We could get ourselves hurt, hunting for stray children in the black of night.'

Just for a moment, I felt tickly hurt. I didn't want him frightened, but I never wanted him to be unbothered either. Uncle Jack was sounding real casual. He really didn't seem to care. I glared out at him. At least the others couldn't see him grinning.

I was just about to give myself up, when I saw him point towards me. At the same time he raised his shushing finger!

Had he spotted me? Me, the Romany who can lie like a newly dropped fawn, quiet and still for hours. I didn't understand, I had hardly breathed. I stared at him, and he stared back at me. I was like a rabbit in torchlight, mesmerised. He shouldn't see me, not lying unbreathing still, not me. I was a Romany. I *couldn't* be the one to be found, not *me*. The silence felt thunderbolt-loud. That hadn't been my plan at all.

He wasn't! He was not looking at me. He was gazing a way in front, where, tucked close to the tree, I had left a neat little line of shoes.

Aunt Emma and Uncle Jack stood side by side. If they heard Penny's cough, or Mary's hiss, they never let on. They stood eye-focused towards the hedge by the tree.

'I thought I heard something,' Uncle Jack said after a while, 'but I think it was only a mouse.'

Aunt Emma took his arm. 'You're right, darling. It's far too dark to look now. We'll call the police when we've had a good look in the morning.'

They walked back towards the house. It was Mary who broke the silence.

'I told you it would be all right. We'll be tucked up safe in the tent in the morning.'

Penny giggled, her hand reaching out to touch mine. Over her head Mary and I shared a satisfied wink.

'Won't Aunt Emma be surprised to see us back, Penny?' I said and we properly laughed ... all together.

I sighed contentedly. Uncle Jack did love me. He'd spotted my sign and he hadn't let on. He'd guessed we were there, and was determined not to spoil things. I'd left a patteran, a sign, just so they shouldn't be cold-heart frightened. I am a proper Romany. I would never be so careless, not with a line of happy-colour shoes.

14 Changeover Time

Aunt Emma's wild garden is a wonderful place. It always surprises me that someone with such tidy ways can open their heart to scatter-plant glory.

Mary and Penny prefer the formal gardens. They like soldier-straight plants, and elegant, flower-dressed trees. Mary often helps Uncle Jack to mow the lawn, or Aunt Emma to prune and trim. I think Penny feels safe in the top garden. She'll sit as still as the big stone statue while all the fine gardening bits go on, but she's much better now. She often helps with the weeding.

It's Tuesday and late, we should all be asleep. Penny is, if tossing and turning is really sleep. Mary is reading a book. Me? I've crept out here. Aunt Emma doesn't worry about me so much now, she knows that I'm Chime-Child wise. Maggie came out with me, but she's gone off late-night food hunting.

She'll come back soon; she's a purple-coated coward, is Magpie.

Soon it will be the changeover time. Those few extra-quiet minutes, where the day turns into night. The birds will stop having their last minute sing-songs that remind each other whose nest belongs to who.

I quietly remove my toes from the still pond water, so as not to disturb the magic silence. I love this moment, especially when I'm quite alone.

Back home, we would hardly notice the change-over time. Tashar or Mam would be kicking the fire into life for their supper-time drinks. Great-gran would want strong sweet tea. Mam would prepare for Dibby Gran a light herbal blend, probably primrose and cowslip to make sure she sleeps like the innocent child she is.

Tashar would need to check the hosses had food and sweet fresh water before the black of night. I expect he's slipped them into a farmer's field, where they can graze and rest till morning.

The dogs – Sabre, Fusty and Woodpile – will settle in their places under the vardo to guard the wagons, tents and carts. By now, our camp will be almost silent, even Vashti will have given up sorting through his endless piles of scrap.

The day jobs complete, Tashar will most likely sneak off through the woods. Sometimes he goes to poach, but mostly he joins up with other Roms for pints of beer, gambling and man-time chatter. At home, by the time that all the work is done, the fox and owl are night-time hunting and the stillness of change time is long-over gone.

Here, this quiet time is so strong that I can mind-think quite easy. Gone are my day child-busy limbs. I sit legs crossed, with my hands resting lightly on my knees. I am not here. I am home with my mam.

'Hello, Chime,' my mam says, her eyes lighting up as she sees me. 'How's things?'

'Slow, Mam. I miss you. I never thought the magic would take so long.'

Mam finishes washing her night-drink cup, and stacks it carefully away. 'I feel like you have been gone a long time,' she admits, 'but not too far. Why, how else could you be here?'

'If I couldn't mind-talk, then I'd be so empty with missing you.'

'Me too,' Mam agrees, shaking her fingers at Dibby Gran, to show that she is serious about wanting her in bed right now.

'Give Dibby a kiss, and Great-ostrich-gran.'

Mam nods. 'Dibbs, Freya wants me to give you

a goodnight kiss from her . . . but not until you're tucked up in bed proper!'

I head-laugh. My mam is smart. She never misses a chance to take advantage. Mary and she are pea-pod made.

'Where's Freya, then?' Dibby Gran asks, as she pulls her quilt up tight round her chin. 'Why can't she kiss me herself?'

'She's busy. Don't you remember how she was called to work by the flames?'

Dibby Gran shakes her head. 'I miss her,' she says, not knowing I am there.

'She'll come back soon,' my mam tells her gently. 'You'll see her soon.' To an outsider things look the wrong way round, for it was Dibby Gran who birthed my mam, and my mam who acts as her mother. Poor Dibby Gran can't help being head-hit damaged. Like Frances Bootle, there was a moment when she didn't think clearly. Her head was dented, and now she will stay childlike for ever. My mam, and my tribe, don't care. Dibbs is still a lovely person. We will take care of her.

I try to make Dibby Gran understand that I am close. I send loving thoughts into her head as strongly as I am able. In a way I succeed. She closes her eyes and whispers, 'I love you, little Chime.'

Satisfied that Dibby Gran is safely sleeping, Mam creeps out of her metal wagon to check up on Great-gran. I go with her. By now Vashti and Tashar and the others are fair-few beers happy. We can hear the men's laughter drifting back through the woods.

'Tashar should have checked her,' Mam mutters, 'but he thinks a passing glance is good enough. You can never trust a man to do a job real proper!' I cannot help but laugh, she is beginning to sound a lot like Great-ostrich-gran.

Great-gran is creaky-bone ancient and, to her, the nights are endless long. Her bed quilts and mattresses are all soft-feather filled, but, even in summer, if she lies still for too long, her body feels winter-cold.

'Not sleeping, Ostrich?'

My mam is wrinkle-brow concerned. Great-gran tries to ease her worry-time lines.

'I'm fine, girl! For goodness sakes, you have no need to worry yourself about me!'

GIRL! How can my mam be a girl? She has to care for absolutely everybody. She, who is now mother to our tribe.

'How long will you sit in that chair?'

Great-gran pulls her shawl tight across her frail

shoulders, more because she is cross than because she is cold. 'Until I'm good and ready to go to bed! Now be a good girl and go back to your little tin house, and keep your nose right out of my business.'

'Ostrich, do your bones ache? I have made you a soothing potion.'

Great-gran glares, and I notice that her don't-miss-a-trick eyes are quite sulky-day cloudy. 'You'll be wanting me tucked up by Dibby next, so you can hover all night over both of us.'

'Well . . .'

'Oh, for goodness sake, child! Give me your potion and go to your bed. A little peace would go down well.'

My mam has the drink already made. She's used primrose and cowslip, just like she did for Dibbs, but she's added some burdock too, to help ease Great-gran's aching bones, and stinging nettle because our Ostrich's skin grows pale, and her eyes have grown almost as big as her head.

It's the same story every night, just like the fights over leaving me the vardo. Great-gran always pretends she doesn't need her medicine. She won't admit that she's feeling frail and creaky-bone old.

Great-gran rocks gently, making the gentle movements that help to slow the stiffening of her bones. As soon as Mam has left, she reaches out to gulp the night-time potion that eases her hotchy-fidgit bone pains and lets her snatch a little sleep.

'Are you there, Chime?'

'I'm here, Great-gran.'

'You're a long time doing that magic, girl!'

'You're not with me to help, are you? You're sitting here, rocking away, when you could be with me, working spells.'

I used my teasing voice, the one I only really learned when I first met Aunt Emma. Sometimes Great-gran gets real cross when I tease, but tonight she just chuckles and smiles.

'I'm glad I have you,' she tells me. 'It's nice to know that the magic will pass on.'

'I'm called. I have no choice.'

Great-gran chuckles again. 'One day, my little Chime Child, one day not so far away, you will sound nearly as grumpy as me!'

In my mind I am hugging her close, so close that I can feel her paper-thin skin, and have to be mindful not to bruise her with caring.

'Will you forgive me, Chime, if I follow the proper way, and have my vardo burned?'

My mind is tumble-tossed. The vardo is home, life, and magic to me. I love it nearly as much as I love my great-gran. If I'm cross-heart truthful, I need that vardo. It's the past, and the future, to me.

'No, of course I don't mind, Great-gran.' I try to keep my voice honest-loud, and my heartbeat tell-truth slow.

'How can I pass over to the happy place, if my wagon is not burned? How can I be sure things are right, if I haven't done them properly?'

Great-gran is the oldest of us all. She is wise beyond our knowing . . . and she is asking me!

I'm torn. My mam thinks different to my great-gran, she's part-ways modern. Me? I think I'm somewhere middling, but in the case of the vardo, I side with my mam.

'You've earned your happy place, Great-gran,' I tell her firmly, desperately hoping that she will believe. 'It will be there . . . no matter what you do.' I look her firmly in the eye. 'But if you have the need, then burn it. I would not want it if it kept you from finding peace.'

The words are hard to say. Great-stubborn-ostrich-gran rewards me with her loving smile, but she still isn't finished. I feel her grip on my arm. 'Would you have it burned it if it was yours? Would you be scared of not reaching the great beyond?'

'No, Great-gran. Never.'

'You young are always mouth-full confident!' She tries to sound cross, but I can tell that she isn't. I kiss her gently, even if it isn't a Romany thing to do. She draws her lip tight, but I can see the happiness tear in her eye.

'Go, child!' She dismisses me, as if our words meant nothing. 'I shall sleep now.'

I am back in Aunt Emma's wild garden. The change-time minutes are over. An owl hoots, a mouse squeals, a passing fox makes the bushes rustle. Maggie-Magpie leaves her place on the branch beside me, and hops closer for comfort. I hold her to me. It is night and I must go back to the house to sleep, but first, if she's wakeful, I'll share a quick cuddle with Briar Rose.

15 Riddles

'What's the matter?'

I woke to find Penny plucking my sheets; her face was all worry-furrowed.

'What's wrong?'

Penny's lips moved but no sound came and, fuggy with sleep, I couldn't read the movements. I yawned and rubbed the sleep-sand from my eyes. It wasn't even nearly normal for me to lie in bed so late, but I had been night-time busy. I had spent all of my dreamtime with my precious great-gran.

I was still being tugged into wakefulness. Penny must be proper upset to shake me so. As soon as she was sure I was watching, she pointed to the carry bag. There was no sign of Maggie-Magpie. She had most definitely gone. I wasn't deep-depressed bothered. Maggie-Magpie was born to be free, that's why I never shut the window that Penny was dragging me so doggedly towards.

I stopped being cross at being woken. On the

other side of the room, Mary was snoring gently, and she was missing the most beautiful of mornings.

Maggie-Magpie was flying slowly round in the pink mist of dawn, her feathers gleaming even to her white feather shawl. Round and round she flew, simply for the joy of being.

'I'd begun to think she'd never leave me,' I told Penny softly. 'I'd almost hoped we'd be together for ever, but she has to be free to choose.'

Penny didn't speak, but she gave me a sympathetic smile as we stood close together, watching the glinting sheen of well-oiled feathers. Maggie looked true-bird beautiful, like a lady in a dark blue satin dress topped by a pure white stole. On her third loop, she paused and headed closer towards the great white maple. She rose high and dived, making her gown seem purple and dressed with jewels. 'She's after something,' I whispered, as she dive-bombed the tree again.

Penny pointed. This morning her big brown eyes were keener than mine. There on the large cross branch was another magpie, a magnificent bird that was making no effort to move. He just sat preening, and pretended not to have noticed my Maggie.

Maggie-Magpie grew more brave. She landed a little further up in the tree. The resident bird still ignored her. He carried on with his morning polish-wash as if she had not been seen, and he didn't squawk; he was button-beak silent.

He head-tilted slightly when she crept closer. He fluffed himself up, as only a magpie can. Having made himself fluff-feather big, he simply stopped pretending to oil his coat and watched.

'It's time Maggie-Magpie had a friend,' I told Penny. 'Let's leave her to it.'

I glanced at my watch. It was far too late to go back to bed, especially on such a beautiful day as this one. I decided to read aloud to Penny in the breakfast room. That way we could share the sun-shine and yet not disturb the magpies. I chose *The Jungle Book*. Uncle Jack says we all live in a jungle, I just like the animal friends. We stayed there, quite content, until it was time to join the others for toast and marmalade.

'Uncle Norman is coming over again today,' Aunt Emma announced brightly as we sipped our early morning tea. 'Would you girls like him to take you to the hospital this time?'

Mary and I looked at Penny. Her hand was clamped tightly round her toast, melting butter ran all down her fingers, the toast curled up in a soggy roll.

'I think she'd rather we go with you, Uncle Jack,' I said firmly. I didn't *think*. I was itching-uncomfortable sure!

'I'll take you then,' Uncle Jack replied calmly. 'But if you change your minds, then that's fine with me . . . only I am rather busy.'

I felt uneasy. There was no reason why we shouldn't go with Uncle Norman, no reason I could fix in my mind. We'd bumped into him at the hospital the very first time we went, the Sunday after the mural-painting.

'Hello, how nice to see you!' he'd said, and vanished to do some urgent task. It seemed that, like his brother, Uncle Norman was always busy.

Frances Bootle had seemed relieved to see him go, but then she was so excited at seeing Penny. First they sat staring uneasily at each other, but then they hugged and kissed and cried. Mary and I had felt quite ukky-awkward, until we were needed to tell Penny's mother everything that had happened since they had last met . . . well, everything happy, that is.

From the first mention of Uncle Norman, Penny had been butterfly-brained. She didn't listen to *half* of what we said. Aunt Emma made cakes for tea and we all helped, but Penny even got that wrong.

She weighed her flour not bothering to look at the numbers, and she dropped an egg. It was a good job we were all keeping an eye on her.

Uncle Norman seemed OK to me, especially when he came to the house loaded down with presents. I'd expected Penny to enjoy getting them, but she was *never* pleased. Usually it was, 'Here's a little something to make you feel better, sweetheart.' It never did. I once heard Aunt Emma telling Uncle Norman that money could never ever buy love, but he never listened, he always came in hope.

This time there were presents for Mary and me too. It was just like Christmas. Uncle Norman wore fewer worry-wrinkles now, he handed me a package, wearing a nice shy smile. He did the same for Mary, and last of all Penny. 'Frances told me how lovely you all were to her,' he said, 'and this is a little thank you.'

'Is it from Mrs Bootle then?' I asked.

'No, sweetheart, Frances can't shop. It's from me.'

'Thank you,' I said, giving him a wide-beam grin. I like presents, and Uncle Norman likes to see the whole world smile, so that's fair. He must be *exactly* like his brother.

I opened my parcel. Inside was a wild-flower

T-shirt, all happiness-bright. 'Thank you, thank you!' I said, and gave him a great gorgio hug, even though I knew Penny was glaring.

Mary's gift was a cornflower-blue blouse, with little dark blue trimmings. I thought it rather dull but she was very pleased indeed. We waited for Penny to open her package. It obviously wasn't clothes. We waited eager-eyed until Aunt Emma reminded her quite firmly of her manners.

Slowly, Penny revealed a beautiful golden-haired doll in ballet-dress clothes. Mary and I gasped. She was tall and elegant and just made to dance. She had big blue eyes that opened and closed, a lacy dress edged with silver sparkles, she even had silken tights and silver shoes. That doll was drop-mouth stunning-wonderful, but we soon realised that it changed nothing. Penny still couldn't stand the sight of Uncle Norman. As soon as she dared, she grabbed my hand and dragged us upstairs to play.

I felt like I was missing out. I was sure that if we'd hung around downstairs, we'd have found out more, but Penny would have none of it.

The only good thing about going upstairs on such a lovely day, was that Maggie was back. She sat on the edge of her carry bag, and greeted us all with a friendly squawk.

'Why, hello!'

Maggie-Magpie flew over and pecked at me in welcome. Without thinking I rubbed her neck with my fingers. 'Stupid bird! Why didn't you take your chance for a mate?' I tried to sound real cross, so she'd feel free to fly away again, but I don't think she was fooled, not for a moment. She just continued to nip gently at my ears. I was double-delighted to see her, despite my fine words.

Penny slung her beautiful doll on the bed. I picked it up, and stroked its golden hair. It was rougher than mine to finger-feel, but still silky. I opened her eyes by tilting her body, and then I let them close. Penny took no notice. She stared out of the window, her mind miles away.

'Why don't you like Uncle Norman?' Mary asked, tired of being tiptoe careful. 'You *have* to have a reason.'

I played with the doll, watching out of the corner of my eye to see what would happen. Mary marched up to Penny and thrust a paper and pen into her hands. 'If you want us to help, then you have to tell us what is going on,' she told Penny firmly.

Penny turned round, wearing crosspatch eyes.

She held up the paper and slowly tore it into long thin shreds, and then, to make sure the job was properly done, she turned the paper shreds round and tore them again. It took quite a long time, the pieces were very small. When she had finished, she threw them at Mary, making her look like a confetti bride.

'So much for the direct approach!' I muttered, adding more loudly, 'I think it is time we had a fresh air walk, don't you?'

Mary, Penny, Magpie and me went out for what Uncle Jack called a constitutional. He says that means there's nothing particular to do, it's just good for you. We pootled off to the rough garden where we had camped, and sat on the edge of the wild garden pond.

Mary and I tried to catch frogs. Penny sat and sulked near by. She was still cross-bunny sullen at being pushed too hard. Mary caught more frogs than me, she'd given up on Penny and was free to have fun. I was trying to head-think, what on earth were we doing wrong?

I only had a few days left before my mam would come back, and Great-gran was getting weaker by the day. I had to mind-think real strong to contact her now. I had to think for her and me.

Great-gran had always helped me with my magic. Sometimes so much that my mam got twitchy-tongued.

'The child would be better making medicine than learning silly spells.'

'Freya is a Chime Child. She has to help when she is called. The magic will help her. There are times when caring is not enough.'

'She spends too much time with you. She should help me more with Dibby.'

'Dibby doesn't need help. She might only have half a brain, but she's always happy. How many of us can say that?'

Great-gran was right about Dibby. She's usually right. She has taught me almost everything she knows, and that's plenty, but day by day I grow more frightened. I am scared stiff that it isn't enough. The time-sands are flowing too fast.

16 An Invitation

'Freya, a moment, please.'

I shrugged at Mary and Penny, before following Aunt Emma into the kitchen where Uncle Jack was shovelling down breakfast, as he often did when he was late. His manners weren't awfully pretty. If I had eaten like him, he would have been very tongue-wag cross indeed.

'We're going to baptise baby Rose this Sunday,' Aunt Emma said, as Uncle Jack glanced up at the clock. I nodded.

'We'd like you to be one godmother, and Aunt Sally the other.'

I nodded again . . . a big heavy happy up-and-down nod.

'And Uncle Jack's brother, Norman, has agreed to be godfather.'

Now I understood why I had been called to the kitchen. Penny would be furious when she was told.

'Why does Penny hate Uncle Norman?'

Aunt Emma handed me a cup of tea and the milk for my cereal. 'I really can't understand why Penny hates Norman,' she said, pushing the sugar towards me at high speed. 'It's not that he hasn't done everything possible to show that he wants to be friends.'

'I agree. I like Uncle Norman, he always seems fine to Mary and me. Will we *all* go to Briar Rose's christening?'

Aunt Emma glanced at Uncle Jack, who was putting some papers into his briefcase and muttering about his busy-bee schedule.

'She's so anti-baby, and anti-Norman, and anti the world. A christening should be a joyful day. Freya, I'm sorry, but I really don't want it spoiled. Is that so very selfish?'

'No, of course not, Aunt Emma,' I said, raising my head so that Uncle Jack could give me a leaving kiss.

'We thought that, just for the christening, Penny should stay at Aunt Sally's. She has a really splendid baby-sitter for the younger ones and, just for one day, Penny will have to stay where she is told.'

'You'll be godmother, then?' Uncle Jack asked as he opened the door. 'Freya, please say that you will.'

159

'I'd love to, Uncle Jack. Really, it will be an honour.' I used my posh voice, so that he should know I was jump-over-the-moon pleased.

Uncle Jack nodded happily as he left, but I called him back. 'Uncle Jack?'

'Yes, Freya?'

'Will she be called *Briar* Rose?'

'Of course she will, sweetheart. It will be rather like a wagon name. We shall baptise her Briar Rose, so she can grow up sweet and slightly wild and remind us of you.'

'Not that we can ever forget!' Aunt Emma teased.

'Her formal name though will simply be Rose . . . is that OK?'

I nodded. It was very OK. A wagon name is a secret thing to be used in the family, not all over the world where anybody can hear.

17 Great-gran

I mind-travelled back to my home. Home to a Romany is not a place, but a family. Within moments, I felt like I had never been away.

Great-gran was being bustle-bossy busy as usual. 'Tashar, I want you to build me a box.'

'What sort of box, Ostrich?'

My big brothers were always allowed to use Gran's wagon name, even though I was told it was a fair bit rude. Tashar had quite forgotten that she had any other name at all.

'How did she get called that?' I'd asked once, when I was nearly baby-small.

'You'll soon learn, Freya, that your great-gran is as stubborn as a mule. She has the ability to put her head right deep into the sand like an ostrich, so she sees only what she *wants* to see. Believe me, Chime Child, our great-gran is very well named indeed.'

'Was she always pig-head stubborn?'

'From the very day that she was born, even Dibby had to do as she was told. When she was a child, if she didn't, she got threatened with a great big stick with a nail in it.'

'Did Great-gran ever beat Dibby?' I asked, finding it hard to imagine her being so cruel.

'No, of course not!' Tashar said, laughing loud enough to wake the world. 'She only threatened. When she pretended to fetch the stick, Dibby stopped playing up. She believed she would . . . every time.'

'Poor Dibby Gran. It must be hard to have a wheel-bashed brain.'

'Not as hard as raising an endless child,' Tashar said, his tone grim. 'Your great-gran *had* to be an ostrich. It was not seeing the problems others found, that helped her to raise Dibby so well.'

We shared a conspiratorial grin. Great-gran might be stuck-mule obstinate, but we both loved her oodles full.

Even though she was now shaky-bone frail, Great-gran still lit the little grey pipe that gave her such pleasure in the evenings. She coughed and spluttered out smoke before bossing out her latest plans.

'Tashar! Get your great bum off the floor. Leave

all that heavy horse stuff, and come and listen to your great-grandmother. I want you to make me a box . . . and I want you to start on it *now*.'

'What sort of box, Ostrich?' Tashar asked, barely looking up from his stitching.

'A funeral box, stupid! What other sort of box would I want after all these years?'

Tashar and I gaped. It was as if we were really seeing our great-gran for the first time in years. Her face was waxy pale beneath her leathery creases. Her eyes stood out like saucers, bright and sunny, but set in rings of black. She had grown shrunk-jumper small.

She's old! I thought, suddenly really seeing her through a stranger's eyes, and I knew that Tashar was as shocked as me, but he was really there, and I was just in dreamtime. I knew I must get real time back soon.

'I'm not going yet, Chime Child!' Great-gran roared, well aware of my plans, when I had thought her almost gone. 'So don't even *think* of letting me down!'

Satisfied that she had button-lipped me, Great-gran turned to my brother. 'Tashar, I tell you it's time you built me the box. The most beautiful box you can. I want it to look just like a vardo. I want it mirror-close similar.'

Tashar's mouth was caught fly-catch open. Great-gran's eyes twinkled in delight. 'Not a moment to lose,' she said, sounding young-girl giggly. 'So get on with it!'

'A fancy box?'

'Yes, you cloth-eared clout, a fancy box. I want the carvings to match the ones on my wagon. I want a feather mattress; find one that is really soft. I want to be treated like a queen. It's about time you youngsters showed me due respect now, isn't it?'

'You have been treated like a queen for endless years. How would we have dared do otherwise? So why should I start on your silly box now?'

'Look with your eyes!' Great-gran ordered, and her frail body quivered. 'Now *build* me that box. It must be ready before the Chime Child has finished her work. I warn you, Tashar. It *must* be ready for then.'

'But, Ostrich . . .'

'A funeral box, Tashar! One that will cause the whole Romany world to chitter-chat for years. Are you listening, boy? Nothing else will do, and there isn't much time, Tash, so get on with it.'

I felt unwelcome tears in my eyes. 'Great-gran,

don't think of dying,' I whispered. 'I love you, besides, I *need* you.'

Great-gran looked me straight in the eyes, even though I wasn't truly there. 'Stupid child! Have faith in yourself. Do you really think that I can live for ever? Look at these crumbling bones . . . don't you think they've seen better days? Must I suffer to death to ease the pain in your heart?'

'But, Gran . . .'

'No buts! Do you think I want to end up stuck in my vardo, unable to even reach out to the sun? Do you? No! I want to die with dignity, lying on fresh-cut straw and staring up at the distant stars. I *want* to leave while life is good.' She grinned, and her voice was teasing again. 'I have to be strong enough to look down so I can keep a good eye on you all. Well, don't I?'

I nodded, understanding. I share her love of open fields, changing woodlands, and fresh sharp morning air. If a door slams shut, the nicest room becomes a prison.

'Well, there you are,' Great-gran said, and she was still smiling. 'I *will* leave long before the cold of winter. I shall die on my back, looking up at the stars, and the family will sing and dance, and make music as loud as they can.'

I nodded, and Tashar nodded. It was best that she chose the time of her passing. We Romanies can do that. We know just when to hand over our souls, but my heart felt sliver-shiver shredded at the very idea of us parting.

18 Shimmering Gold

I had done my hand-on-heart best to make Penny every bit better. I had struggled so hard, and failed.

Maggie-Magpie and I sat alone in Aunt Emma's wild bit of garden. It was not yet dawn and the rest of the house was sandman-sleeping.

I closed my eyes, and wished that I was home with my mam and my grumpy old great-gran. I was tumble-tummy sick of missing them so much.

There was something missing from my magic, something important. I just couldn't think what to do next, no matter how hard I tried.

'*This silk is a link,*' I had told Penny, threading her much-loved handkerchief through the wedding ring that my great-great-gran had given me at birth. It wasn't her wedding ring. It was the one that *her* great-grandmother had given to her. It was *ages* old, it carried generations of love. It was the next best thing to the teardrop crystal, but it was impossible to thread a silk through that.

I dipped my undressed toes into the cold pond water. It was moody-soup black in the near-night darkness. Maggie-Magpie nudged my ear, as if to remind me that sensible creatures should still be glue-stuck shut-eyed.

'*This ring is a joining,*' I whispered, wishing that I had succeeded in unlocking Penny's troubled mind. We had been bonded but still I couldn't free her chilled-chatter tongue.

I swirled my toes in the water, and this time the ripples glistened in the first kiss of the morning dawn.

'*This touching is a bond between Penny and me.*' I tried to believe that the bond between us was powerful, a strong bridge, and I simply needed to find the way to cross.

Penny mourned for Katya, and because of that despised the world, especially Uncle Norman. I felt weary-world worried – the great god Arivell had been known to feed on the seeds of hatred. I pleaded with Moshto to keep her safe.

Maggie-Magpie grew restless as I sat. Now it was almost bright enough to see, she let out a raucous squawk. The noise was ear-shake loud. I brushed her away; she was too early and *I* needed the silence of morning.

Maggie grew fluff-feather cross. She came back and gave me a big defiant ear peck. Again, I shoved her away. This time she flew sulkily off towards the house.

I rested my chin on my knees. Maggie was grown-up now, and she had a stubborn mind all of her own. I shouldn't have shoved her. At the moment, I needed her more than she needed me.

I dug deep in my pocket and pulled out my teardrop crystal. It glowed pink in the gently warming dawn.

I needed the safeness of home. Back by the wagons, everything is normal. Dibby Gran is gathering feathers with the young chavis, she who will never have need of a marriage bed. Despite her middle years, she picks them up gleefully and dries and saves them with pride.

Not far away, Great-gran and Mam are talking in the vardo. They smile down at my dibby gran now and then, sometimes gently teasing as she proudly shows them each downy plume she finds. '*Another* feather, Dibbs, you are such a *clever* girl!'

Mam and Great-gran are drinking herbal tea. They've been up and busy for hours, even if it is early in the morning. Great-gran can't be too busy-fingered now, but she still likes to think she's doing her very best to help.

Tashar, my closest prala, isn't about. I expect he's abandoned the box, and is dealing horses somewhere. I guess my other brothers are with him. They all enjoy an excuse to talk and trade.

Dibby is soon bored with feathers. She creeps close to the cooking fire. Mam is down from the vardo in a flash. She grabs Dibbs and leads her towards our big metal caravan. 'Come, Dibby, shall you be a big girl, and help me dry the herbs while our Chime is away?' Mam wants to keep Dibbs safe, so together they leave the dancing flames.

Great-gran finishes her tea. The camp is quiet. Rattle-pot Great-gran is soon silent-time bored.

'I miss you, Chime,' she says out loud.

'I miss you, Great-gran,' I mind-think back. 'I miss you a million trillions.'

Great-gran chuckles as she slowly climbs the steps back up to her happy-colour vardo to fetch her heavy-fringed shawl, and then comes down again. 'I wish you were here, Chime. I could do with your help with the horses.'

'I can't break the bonding bridge, Great-gran,

170

you trouble-told me that, but I think I shall be glue-stuck here for ever.'

'Stop being a worry-bones, Freya. The bridge grows strong with trust. You'll find the key soon.'

'I don't know what to do.'

'Listen to your heart and the magic will come to you.'

She's walking towards the hoss and pony. Her bones are weary, but her mind is still sharp. 'I love you, Ostrich!' I whisper aloud.

'I love *you*, Chime Child,' she calls as she fades, and I am back all alone in the first warm wrap of morning.

Maggie sensed my return, and flew back from the shade of the house. This time her crazy chatter succeeded in breaking the sweet peace.

'Shut up, Maggie-Magpie.'

Maggie ignored me, so I kicked the water, it splashed up in the air, and all over my silly bird. She shook her feathers and a thousand droplets twinkled in the morning sun. Maggie flew higher. I kicked harder but this time, the iridescent spray couldn't reach her. Maggie arched round over my twinkle-water cloud, and suddenly dropped something she'd been holding in her beak.

Penny's silver sixpence tumbled towards the

wild-pond water. Penny's silver sixpence, Katya's only gift to her older sister.

Instinctively, I reached out my hand, catching the spinning coin mid-fall. My heart, which had stopped in the losing fear, breathed easy with relief. To Penny, the silver sixpence was the most valuable thing on earth.

I opened my hand. The sixpence glistened. I closed my fingers round it tight and, after a moment, when I was sure it was safe, I opened my hand again. Still the little coin shone, wrapped in its sprinkle-water coat.

The sun was now warm and golden; it reflected from the moistened surface of the gleaming silver. It turned the silver into gold.

Maggie-Magpie flew to my shoulder, climbed down to my hand, and pecked the coin . . . peck peck.

I ignored her. In my head I was thinking. I knew I was close to the bridge key. I could even see my great-gran, and she was nodding and smiling.

Peck peck.

I curled my fingers to stop my little coin thief. As I curled my hand, the coin changed back, from bouncy gold to softer silver . . . peck peck. Three pecking times, three chains, three children, a sunlit sixpence and some shining mirror water.

I sat hardly daring to breathe, the answer was so close. I was the link, the bond in the magic. Mary was closest to the gorgio gods, she knew lots about holy water. Water had turned the silver sixpence into shimmering gold. Penny's sixpence memento from her sister. Maggie had warned me three times, that the answer lay right in my palm.

As I inspected the little coin again, the answer came to me. 'Thanks, Great-gran!' I yelled, leaping to my feet. 'Thanks for everything.'

'I did *nothing*,' Great-gran's voice echoed back across the garden. 'You don't think that *I* would ever dream of working magic with that stinky old bird!'

I didn't believe her, but it didn't matter. Somehow I had discovered the key. It was the healing magic of gold and silver water.

19 Holy Water

'Mary, you've got to help me.'

Mary looked up from her jigsaw. 'I'm here, aren't I? I've put up with Penny's odd little ways for weeks, and your even stranger notions. I've been the constant companion to a pair of real weirdos, and now nothing will surprise me. Freya, before you tell me your next madcap idea, get that damn bird away from my pieces.'

'Will you steal some holy water?'

'What!' Mary's face went white as a sheet, and she almost tipped up her puzzle. 'You *are* joking . . . aren't you?'

'Well, I see I can still surprise you,' I told her, putting in two pieces and ignoring her warning glare. 'Mary, I do need your help . . . please.'

Mary said nothing. She took out one of my pieces and added two more.

'Penny can't word-speak because she needs

magic done with holy water. I can't manage that all on my own, so I need you to help me.'

'Oh, big deal. You need holy water and I get to steal it. I thought you had ancient gods of your own. Haven't I heard you rambling on about Soster, Moshto and Arivell? Weren't they supposed to control the wonders of the world?'

'They're ancient gods. This magic is tickle-brain difficult. We need help from the new gods too.'

'Not *that* new!' Mary said drily. 'But obviously not as worn out as yours.'

I scowled. 'It's simply that the more help we get, the better.'

'It's simply that your gods are not good enough,' Mary said, giving me her most triumphant smile.

She was wrong, but it was no time to argue. I shrugged. 'So will you help?'

'Where's Penny been?' Mary asked, giving herself thinking time.

'Getting changed, Aunt Emma's just taken her to the dentist. Her face is boiled-egg swollen. Have you been so busy with that jigsaw you couldn't see? Maggie! No! Don't you *dare*!'

'Can't say I noticed,' Mary admitted, waving her arms to try and frighten Maggie-Magpie off. 'I

175

was enjoying a time without minding Pudding Pot Penny.'

'Well, now they're back Aunt Emma will go shopping with baby Rose. She hasn't had a proper fresh-air push to make her sleep. Uncle Jack won't be home for ages, so Penny will be shadow-close.'

'And you want me to steal holy water *now*?' Mary asked, not even bothering to look up from her jigsaw to greet Penny.

'No, silly, it has to be blessed before it becomes holy water. First we have to collect it from the south-running stream.'

'Oh, of course!' Mary said, resting the box on her half-finished puzzle. 'Fancy me not realising that the water had to be from a south-running stream. Freya, why can't you ever do things the easy way?'

'So will you come?'

'I suppose so!'

Outside, the wind was hot swirly mad. It made us tumble-warm with summer gladness. The leaves in the trees around us made frothy waterfall noises. Gusty spurts of hotness bathed our faces and tried their best to trip us over.

Even Mary was impressed. She stood on her toes and closed her eyes. The windy wraps rocked her gently. 'Penny, have a go at this.'

Penny stood next to Mary and let herself be wind-rocked too. It was breezy-rock fun. Penny smiled and giggled as she joined in. The windy wraps were strong and warm. It was like we were in hot-air cradles. Luckily, after a while, the wind dropped, or I might never have persuaded them to help me fetch the water.

'This is a south-running stream.'

'Oh good!' Mary said, raising her head and winking at Penny.

'A south-running stream is the best for healing magic.'

'Naturally,' Mary said without a hint of a smile. '*Obvious*.' She picked up a stick and threw it into the gushing water. We watched it get tangled up in tight little current swirls. Penny still rocked on her toes, her arms stretched out wide in the hope of trapping the last bit of whistling wind. *She* was still lost in a magic world of her own.

'If I collect some of this water,' I said, throwing my stick after Mary's, 'do you think you could swop it for the water the priest takes to the church in his carry can?'

'What if I get caught?' Mary asked, tipping Maggie off her shoulder and watching her fly straight to Penny's.

'You won't get caught! He always uses a small white bucket thing. Aunt Emma has one for picnics. We can swop them over,' I said, as Maggie-Magpie left Penny, and flew back to me.

'Oh, that sounds really *simple*,' Mary muttered, giving me her best withering glare. 'You and that bird are playing witches again.'

'He always brings it to the church,' I continued, totally ignoring her gibes, 'one hour before the service. I've seen him do it when I've come with Aunt Emma on flower-arranging duties. He puts the carry bucket by the radiator to warm the water up. Then, Aunt Emma says, just before the service, he puts it in the font.'

'Oh, no problem then,' Mary said sarcastically as we scrambled down the bank. I stood in water that was so high it almost wetted my knickers. Mary balanced on the slippy mud bank that was long slopy deep, and grabbed the bucket from my hand. Penny waited on the safe flat grass at the top, and carried the bucket to safety. Even Maggie-Magpie helped. She dipped, dived and danced all above the fastest running bit, so we were sure our water had the strongest powers.

Penny didn't need to know why we needed the water, but we told her anyway. We wanted her to understand how very hard we were working to make her better.

'By the way, how do I explain about going to Rose's christening service with a white water bucket as a handbag?'

'You don't! We hide it in the churchyard before the day. You swop our water for his before the service, and then . . .'

'Oh, I get it!' Mary said. 'You have a fun christening, and I get myself into a whole lot of trouble.'

'Not at all!' I told her, as we watched my stick get all tangled up in the weed. 'I have the difficult bit. I have to make sure that nobody notices you do all those things *and* I have to be godmother.'

'You can't be a *proper* godmother,' Mary said. 'You're not confirmed, you're not *even* baptised.'

'As far as Aunt Emma and Uncle Jack are concerned, I *am* her godmother. The vicar's happy. He says Aunt Sally can have the formal bit, and he'll say something extra just for me. He says if I promise to care for her gorgio ways, then any *loving* God won't mind.'

20 Sweet Roses

'Oh, do stop dawdling,' Aunt Emma said, impatient to make sure that the flowers were exactly arranged before Rose's baptism.

'I wish Maggie could be here,' I said, sure that if I had her on my shoulder the butterflies in my tummy would go.

'Birds are as welcome in church as they are in kitchens,' Aunt Emma told me primly. 'It's quite nice to have one day without your noisy feathered friend. Now don't you forget, she stays in the garden until all our visitors are gone.'

While we were talking, Mary slipped quietly away. Aunt Emma was so busy being magpie boring that she never even noticed. 'I really can't understand why you cling on to that smelly old bird. She's quite capable of looking after herself now.'

'I don't!' I told Aunt Emma. 'Maggie clings on to me.'

'Uncle Jack will be here with Rose soon,' Aunt

Emma said, changing the subject to safer things. 'I want to make sure that the flowers are perfect. I filled the church with roses last night. It seemed right. A few of them might have wilted.'

'They will be perfect,' I assured her, and in that moment found the inspiration that I needed. 'Have you brought your snipping scissors?'

Aunt Emma pointed to her new green handbag. 'In there.'

I raised my eyebrows, just like she did when she thought that I had done something odd.

'Well, the roses might need trimming,' Aunt Emma told me sheepishly.

'The roses need one more thing,' I said, spotting the vicar glance towards the door that Mary had come through . . . 'Reverend Plumpton! How nice to see you again.'

The vicar turned his attention towards me. 'Hello, Freya, and how are you on such an important day?'

'I'm fine, Mr Priest, but I'll be even better if you let me do something really important.'

The Reverend Plumpton and Aunt Emma waited expectantly.

'Please can you help me cut a proper briar rose?'

'A *briar* rose?'

'Yes, that pretty flower climbing up the hedge over there.'

'It's a bit high.'

'Please.' I offered them my best smile. 'It's a briar rose for my godchild Briar Rose.'

'It does seem a very nice idea,' Aunt Emma said slowly, and already her fingers were undoing the clasp of her nice new handbag.

We made our way carefully, and oh so slowly – which really wasn't me – across the churchyard towards the briar rose.

Aunt Emma was slightly behind, being even more careful. She didn't want a scrap of grass or mud on her matching silk shoes.

The Reverend Plumpton, mindful of his duties, looked torn. He turned to check that no early parishioners had arrived and were waiting to greet him. We were miles early, the place was all people-empty, he relaxed, and decided to follow too. I sighed with relief. Nobody had said, 'Where's Mary?'

The briar grew tall. It was our special baby's christening so we had to have the best rose, even Aunt Emma was agreed on that. She tried to reach up to cut the delicate flower, but the greenery came too close to her very best dress, so she edged away. She offered the Reverend Plumpton her most pathetic smile. I could still learn a lot from Aunt Emma!

To our joy, the Reverend Plumpton smiled sympathetically. He took the tiny scissors from Aunt Emma's gloved hand, reached tall, and picked the most beautiful briar rose.

'Is that the one?'

'It's perfect, vicar, thank you *so* much.'

'Can I carry it into church, please?'

Aunt Emma nodded.

'And will you arrange it in the flowers by the font that will baby-bless?' I asked and Aunt Emma nodded again.

I sniffed the rose, letting its perfume flood my head with smell. 'This will make it a really special baptism,' I told them. 'Thank you so much for letting her have a wagon-naming rose.'

The Reverend Plumpton patted my head. 'I'm glad you realise the importance of today, Freya. That's a beautiful red dress. I expect it's your very best.' I nodded and gave him a twirl so its delicate golden flower threads shone in the sun.

'Well, it's certainly her brightest!' Aunt Emma said, not liking to admit she had spent hours trying to make me wear a more suitable blue, but she bent down to give me a kiss anyway. I gave them my happiest smile. 'I shall like being godmother,' I told them proudly.

'Come on, you lot! I've been waiting for ages!' Mary called impatiently, as if she had been standing on the church path for ever.

'You could have come too,' I teased.

Mary could never be flummoxed. 'What, and spoil my shoes?' she said prissily. 'Just to look at a little wild rose?'

Aunt Emma inspected her own shoes. To my relief, they were still shiny clean. Mine were a hint scruffy. I wiped them on the back of my leg when she wasn't looking.

'The briar rose is important to us, as it is to Freya,' Aunt Emma told Mary as we made our way up the church path. 'They're sweet-scented, beautiful, and a little bit wild and prickly. We Hemmingways are quite convinced that that is not a bad description of Freya!'

Mary laughed. 'Well, the prickly bit is right,' she said.

The parishioners were arriving in earnest now. We left them to the vicar, and followed Aunt Emma through the wooden doors and into church. Mary went off to save us a pew. She settled herself down, and I knew she had half an eye on our hidden swop bucket.

The vase of flowers by the font looked perfect already. I knew it would be spoilt if we changed a single bit. I chewed my tongue, and waited for an idea to rush into my head.

The font was made of soft peach stone and stood on a big plinth. Halfway up was a small ledge, where the column came outwards and then back inwards, like a sort of giant waisted vase.

'We could lay it on the ledge.'

'Will that be good enough?' Aunt Emma asked, her face wide-eyed surprised.

'One single rose will look just right. Anyway, it's the closest flower to the holy water so that's got to be good.'

I laid the flower stalk across the ledge, and it looked lovely. We were both pleased-face happy.

'There, see, it has just a hint of wildness, but it's gossamer delicate.'

'You're right, Freya! It's absolutely perfect.' Aunt Emma wrapped her arms around me.

'Gypsies don't go gooey,' I told her.

'Yes, I know that,' Aunt Emma said, still smiling, 'and if you're anything to go by, they're not too good at sitting still in church either.'

21 The Christening

The baptism took itchy-feet hours long. Mary and I sat beside Aunt Emma and Uncle Jack, trying to look as if such a boring service was fun. Baby Rose was sitting on Aunt Emma's knee all through the morning service that came before her special bit. She was lucky, Aunt Emma had brought a bouncing teddy to keep *her* amused.

Mary and I had nothing to do, except listen to long churchy prayers and badly sung hymns. We had big bubbly butterflies in our tummies, and all the loud singing in the world couldn't drive them away.

Briar Rose's christening was important, of course it was, but my gods, Soster, Moshto and Arivell, were just as good as hers. The holy water was the thing that really mattered. It was the holy water that would help to give Penny her speaking voice.

At long last, just as our knees were sitting-still bouncy, the baptism began. Reverend Plumpton gathered us all round his big stone font, and the whole congregation turned to watch.

'Dearly beloved, for as much as all men are conceived and born in sin . . .' Mary giggled and I frowned. I wasn't born in sin, not me! I was birthed in sweet soft hay, in a special tent that was put up just for me. No! There was no sin about when I came into the world.

Uncle Jack had had a turn holding baby Rose, and now he handed her back to Aunt Emma. The two of them stared at her all starry-eyed. You'd almost believe that they'd never seen the baby before.

'Let us pray. Almighty and everlasting God . . .' I sighed. I was stuffed to the gills with being bored, even if it was a very special posh-frock day.

'They brought young children to Christ, that he should touch them . . .' Aunt Emma and Uncle Jack had given me a book. Inside was a lovely picture of Jesus holding out his arms to the little children. He had long brown hair and friendly eyes. He looked very nice indeed, but I bet his magic was just the same as ours. I wondered if he was in church with us now, and if his arms were reaching out to our baby, Briar Rose.

'Dearly beloved; ye have brought this child to be baptised . . .' At last the vicar was going to magic our south-running stream into holy water. I smiled as the Reverend Plumpton turned to us. 'I demand therefore, dost thou, in the name of this child, renounce the devil and his works?'

I glanced across at Mary and winked. She winked back as, at long last, the priest took Briar Rose into his arms.

'Name this child.'

'Briar Rose.'

My heart was bubble-burst happy! I clutched Mary's hand and, just for a few moments, the need to steal holy water was quite forgotten.

'Briar Rose, I baptise thee in the name of the Father . . .' Holy water was lifted in the Reverend Plumpton's palm and poured gently over Briar Rose's head. She didn't cry, she just stared at him wide-eyed.

'And of the Son . . .' He scooped up more of the precious holy water and puddle-poured it. This time, Briar's mouth puckered and she didn't look too happy. I expect the water was shivery-spine cold, even if it had stood by the radiator for almost an hour.

'And of the Holy Ghost . . .' Reverend Plumpton intoned, wetting the baby's head for the third and last time.

Briar Rose yelled real loud! She was high-spirit wild, as well she should be. Aunt Emma and Uncle Jack looked embarrassed. Mary laughed out loud. 'She's renouncing the devil,' she whispered, her voice ringing crystal clear in the echo-silent church. 'She's renouncing the devil, and *that*'s good!'

'We receive this child into the congregation of Christ's flock . . .' the Reverend Plumpton continued, as if Mary had never spoken. He made the sign of the cross on Briar Rose's forehead. 'And do sign her with the sign of the cross . . .'

Everyone was smiling now, Aunt Emma, Uncle Jack, everybody. The place was happiness filled. Aunt Sally turned her head towards me and winked. I winked back. Somehow, having Briar Rose properly christened made the parsley magic complete. I was glad Aunt Emma had chosen her for a godmother too.

There were a few more prayers and a blessing. I didn't listen too carefully. Mary and I had taken our chance to creep to one side of the long wooden pew. 'I forgot to bring a cup to scoop the water,' Mary mouthed. 'What shall we do?'

I glanced round the little stone church. The font was baby shallow; there was no way that we would be able to scoop the water up with a bucket. I closed my eyes. 'Gorgio Jesus, I need help. Please help us make Penny mouth-speak.' When I opened them again, the congregation was rising, everybody was clapping and smiling and rushing over to admire the new church baby. I suddenly realised that I couldn't see Mary.

I stared at the holy water. The water that the vicar and Briar Rose had magicked. I dipped my fingers in the font and let the droplets trickle through my fingers.

Some people were leaving, but Aunt Emma and Uncle Jack were still being mobbed by villagers.

For the moment I was forgotten, and I felt as lost as I looked.

'It's no good *waiting* for a miracle,' Mary said, appearing from nowhere. 'You have to go and *find* one!'

'Have you found one?'

'In a way.' Mary's voice was triumphant as she drew her hands from behind her back and produced a golden chalice. 'I've been walkabout! Here you are, a small miracle.'

I fetched our white bucket from its hiding-place, and scooped up some of the water as fast as I could.

'Be careful!' Mary warned. 'That little cup is worth millions.'

I scooped the holy water more carefully, being sure not to scratch the shiny metal. At last I was done. 'I'll distract them again; you hide the bucket.' Mary nodded and rushed away while I went back to chat to my gorgio family. Mary didn't return. I'd only expected her to be gone for minutes.

'Where's Mary?'

'Looking for her bracelet. She dropped it in the churchyard somewhere.' I crossed my fingers behind my back to ease the lie. Briar Rose grizzled, and Aunt Emma rocked her. 'The baby's getting hungry. I hope she gets back soon.'

More minutes passed, more long minutes.

'I'll find her,' Uncle Jack said. 'We can't stand here for ever.'

'I'll come too,' I said desperately, and followed them into the churchyard.

The gods were with us again. Mary appeared from behind the great yews. 'You found your bracelet then?' I called, not finding it difficult to make my voice relieved.

I'll say this for Mary, she's quick. 'Sorry it took so long to find, I think I must have been looking for ages!' I hoped her fingers were crossed too. We had managed to tell an awful lot of lies on such a holy day.

We had to be good all through Sunday lunch. The house was full of chitty-chatty visitors. When we had helped to wash up, we were sent out for an hour to play.

There was no time to lose. We raced across to the churchyard to collect our precious water.

'It's even better now!' Mary told me smugly. 'I've been dying to tell you for ages.'

'Why?'

'The vicar gave it an extra blessing. He did one specially for Penny.'

I gape-mouthed at my closest friend. 'How on earth did you manage that?'

'He saw me put the chalice back. He spotted me wiping it dry on my skirt. He said he knew about the bucket and he wanted to know why.'

'So you told him about Penny?'

Mary nodded. 'I told him I had a crazy gypsy friend who needed holy water so that she could work her magic, who was mad enough to believe that, with it, she could make Penny better.'

'And what did he say?'

'He said faith could work miracles in any culture. He blessed the water again, and wished you well.'

'So now we have three-times-strong water, south-running, and double-blessed. Oh, Mary! You have done so fantastically well, surely our magic will work now.'

Mary smiled and I gave her a hug. Penny could be sure that we were doing our very best to make her properly chitter-chatter-mouthed.

22 Church Walk

'We have to wait for the night of the full moon. We'll go to the church on the night that leads into Tuesday.'

'How can we sneak out without being spotted? You know that Aunt Emma has ears like a bat?'

I nodded. That had worried me too, but then I had remembered that I was a Romany, and a Chime Child at that. There were plants that could do anything, and I knew them all.

I took advantage of a game of hide-and-seek. I could hide almost anywhere, it always took ages for the others to find me. Once alone, I took out my love-worn teardrop crystal, just so I could feel cuddle-up close to my mam.

'I need help, Mam,' I said, not needing the crystal to talk like she did, but to clutch like a well-loved teddy. 'Mam, you must help so I can come home.'

'Great-gran sends her love with mine,' Mam said. 'She is growing very frail now, Chime dear, but you are not to worry. She is still light-heart happy in her head. She says you are a fine girl, and she is sure you are doing your magic well.'

'Mam, I need lady's slipper, primrose and feverfew. I need lots of feverfew.'

'Goodness, child, do you wish the world to sleep?'

I laughed. 'Only Aunt Emma and Uncle Jack, oh and Briar Rose too. Mary, Penny and I shall work our magic on the Monday's moon. We need to leave the house sleeping. Mam, as it's too late for fresh spring herbs can you send me our dried ones? Domino is a fast-footed horse, could you send someone on him?'

I felt guilty. My mam and my great-gran were sore-feet miles away and yet it would be impossible for me to buy the herbs we needed here. 'Please, Mam, can you help?'

'To get you home soon, Freya, I would do *anything*. Someone will call tomorrow selling baskets and clothes-pegs. She'll slip you the herbs that you need. Tonight Great-gran will blend them carefully. She says she knows exactly what proportions you need. Our weak old Ostrich is smiling, Chime, you know how she loves making magic things!'

'I miss you, Mam. Give my love to everyone.'

'Do they still treat you kindly?'

I nodded. 'They treat me as their own. I have everything a gorgio girl could want,' I sighed, 'but I am a Romany and I need to run wild. Oh, Mam! I long for the moment when I can be set free.'

Mam nodded, behind her I could just make out the figure of Great-gran. She was huddled in her chair, wrapped in a blanket despite the evening sun. I blew her a kiss. To my relief, I was rewarded with her laughing eyes and crooked smile.

A gypsy called Emeldia came the following day, exactly as agreed. Although she was not of our tribe, she was still very much one of us. Her face was weather-worn wrinkled, her scarf red-flashed with gold. She gave me the herbs, a travelling stone, and a bit of lucky heather. 'Good fortune, Freya,' she whispered. 'Be lucky.'

'Take back my love,' I said, stroking Domino. 'And I'm sorry if I made you bottom-bump weary.'

'What me? Never.' Emeldia was smiling, happy because Aunt Emma had bought two of her pretty baskets and some clothes-pegs, saying that she was quite convinced that wooden clothes-pegs were the very best in the world. I'm sure Aunt Emma was telling the truth and not just being nice to a stranger.

On the Monday night I made an infusion of herbal tea, and persuaded Aunt Emma and Uncle Jack to drink a whole cup each. 'It is important,' I said. 'It will bring you full-heart happiness.'

When they were sandman-sleeping, I crept into the nursery and put a few drops of my infusion on to the little heart-shaped lips of baby Briar Rose. I was very careful to put just enough to make her sleepy, and not a bit more. Briar Rose meant everything to me, even more than Mary and Penny.

They would sleep well now, this gorgio family that I had learned to love so much. They would never for one moment suspect that Mary, Penny and me had been out until early morning.

The magic-key time had come at last. Mary, Penny and I crept out of the sleep-locked house. Uncle Jack was deep-throat snoring, Aunt Emma was heavy-sleep snuffling, and even baby Briar Rose whistled slightly as she slept.

The walk to the church was short but creepy. We decided to cross the garden. It was safer than daring to use the night-time streets.

I had borrowed a torch. We needed it despite the round-faced moon. The path was narrow in the wild-grown garden, and the yews cast dancing shadows across our nervous paths. Somewhere, an owl hooted and half-scared Penny to death. Mary and I had to hold her real tight before she started walking again.

The hardest bit was climbing the fence by the ancient old yews. It was dark and dangerous. By now we were so busy being careful not to fall that we quite forgot to be scared. One by one, we tumbled into the vicarage garden, even Maggie, who was in my carry bag as she wasn't too keen on night-time flying.

'Why on earth did you have to bring that bird?'

'She's part of the magic too.'

'What part?'

'Well, she gave me the idea, and I'm sure she'll be useful somewhere.'

Mary shrugged. Penny looked puzzled. She couldn't mouth-speak but her expression joined in.

We trekked across the vicarage garden, being careful not to make a noise and wake the Plumptons as we passed. Now and then an owl hooted, a fox scurried, or a rat rustled, but apart from that the world slept. Quietly we opened the little gate at the side of the vicarage garden and entered the churchyard proper.

'Now we have to get into the church.'

'The door's locked,' Mary said as I tried it. Penny and I looked troubled.

Brilliant Mary served us well again. She'd already solved the problem of the church-door key.

'He leaves it on the ledge, the one to the left of the door arch.' If her face held a hint of smugness, it was well earned. I had been furrow-headed worried about finding a way to get inside the little stone church.

'It's silly really,' Mary added. 'Anyone could find it if they really looked. It really isn't a sensible place at all!'

'How did you find out?' I asked, quite sure that most people wouldn't see the key on such a high ledge.

'I saw him stretch up to open the church and take the water in to fill the font for Rose.'

Mary showed us the ledge and reached up. It was far too high. I climbed on to her back but there was no chance at all of reaching the key.

'What shall we do now?'

There was only one thing I could think of. I dug in my carry bag, and pulled out the sleeping magpie.

'Come on, little bird. It's your turn to be important again. Fetch the key.'

Maggie looked at me with sleepy eyes, and Mary and Penny laughed.

'Please please, Maggie, fetch me the key.'

I closed my eyes, and stretched out my hands. I thought of the key, imagining it being picked off the too-high ledge and being dropped into my hand. I pictured it moving every bit of the way. I used all my mind-thinks, just imagining the moving key.

I opened my eyes and stared into Maggie's, and then I thought all of the moving again, but this time with my eyes wide open.

Maggie-Magpie stared at me for a long time. Mary and Penny stood perfectly silent. It was as if they sensed I was doing something really important.

Just as I realised that Maggie was too scared of the dark to fetch the key, Mary shone the torch up at the ledge. Instantly Maggie-Magpie followed its light path. She grasped the heavy key in her beak. It was too heavy to fly with. She flapped her wings but still couldn't lift it.

Mary, Penny and me stood heart-stopped silent. I still held out my hands. Maggie-Magpie tugged at the key for endless seconds, then, all of a sudden, she managed to dislodge it. She gave me a bright-eyed look to show me she knew she was clever, and tipped the key off the ledge and into my waiting hands.

We sighed with relief. Maggie flew down to my shoulder. Mary swung open the old wooden door, and the four of us sneaked all soft-footed into church.

23 Trinity Magic

The church was night-time chill. Penny, Mary and I sat side by side. We sat close to keep warm. Our only light was a candle that we had lit before the eastern window.

At one point I sensed footsteps. I ignored them, somehow understanding that they held no threat to me.

The three of us held hands, but I wasn't there. I was back by the campfire with our Romany women. The men were further off, way over on the other side. They were smoking and drinking, while the women were talking and pretending to sew. It all looked normal, but it wasn't. There were far more Romanies than normal, some had travelled for weeks hoping to arrive in time. They were all waiting.

The talking was low-voiced, but not unhappy. Long-past memories were being shared, and new gossip passed. Great-gran was laid on a bed of

202

straw. She was sheltered on one side by the fire warmth, and on the other by her vardo. The night was cool and just a little damp, but no coldness reached her bones. The stars twinkled high in the sky. It was just as she wanted. The night was perfect for us all.

To Great-gran, it appeared that the star lights were drawing closer, getting ready to carry her home. She was full-mind-feeling peaceful. It was the same here, with Mary, Penny and me.

'I wish I'd called Chime,' my mam was saying. 'She should be here with us now.'

Great-gran opened the eyes that had seemed so heavy with sleep. She reached out and touched Mam's hand. 'Don't worry,' she said, 'don't worry for Chime. She's here with us now, just like I promised. It's just that you are too sad to see.'

'Are you sure?'

'I am with her, and she is with me. How else could it be?' Great-gran told my mam, and her voice was real-firm sure, though her thin arms trembled as she reached out for her hand.

'What are we waiting for?' Mary asked.

'I don't know,' I said, irritable at being called

back to the real-time church world. 'I only know that the magic is coming.'

Penny sat between us. She seemed not the least bit worried by the silence of the night. Her shoulders were comfy-slumped, not slightly tensed as was usual. It was Mary and I that felt tight-impatience wrapped.

Only I with my prying bat-ears heard the Reverend Plumpton pattering around the church, as if he was not sure whether to leave well alone or be poky-nose curious. I had no choice but to trust that the time had come, and that, whatever happened, the gold and silver magic would break our joining bond.

On the altar sat the little crystal dish that I had chosen. Normally it would have been used for baby Briar's flowers. Mary's special holy water filled it one-third full. In the water was the sixpence. The silver sixpence that was a present from Katya.

The rising sun crept up to the great eastern window. The patterned picture panels glowed with the first signs of morning. We watched, and we waited. There was nothing else we could do.

The silver sixpence glinted as the rising sun let little rays of light get trapped in the crystal vase.

They travelled down, right through Mary's holy water, until they landed on the silver sixpence.

The magic must start soon. We were all of us here. It was time. At long last, it was time.

Slowly the silver sixpence grew brighter, beginning to glow with the first light of the morning sun. The sun lit the window too, turning the little panes magic mosaic-coloured. Only one ray was hitting our crystal vase, but it was a special light. It was the very first strike of morning.

'Yellow yolk to morning-sun gold,' I whispered, ignoring Mary and Penny's puzzled stares, and the face that flashed at a side window.

'White bright of silver shining sixpence.'

I thought of Briar Rose and her Trinity egg as I intoned my magic. Trinity potions are strong enough to protect us all.

> 'Yellow yolk to morning-sun gold,
> White bright of silver shining sixpence,
> Safety shell, our holy water,
> Trinity of gold and silver water,
> Please make our Penny perfect-made.'

I spoke the words carefully. The magic *had* to work.

We had done everything right. We had made gold and silver water.

Mary, Penny and I watched our shimmering glass. It grew brighter and more and more iridescent. It vibrated with the first gold strike of morning. The power of the light grew. Suddenly that's all there was: just light. Bright white head-splitting light that mind-trapped us all.

'Look!' Penny whispered, grasping my hand.

We watched, open-mouthed, the three of us and Magpie.

There, right in the shiny brightness, stood my great-gran. Her face was spring-healthy brown, and her wise old eyes were twinkling with happiness.

In her arms, she held the baby Katya, all wide-eyed and smiling. Katya had pudgy arms and legs, and her tiny feet were perfect-toe small. There were no broken bits anywhere. She was entirely whole.

My great-gran had a little girl holding her other hand, and suddenly I realised that the giggling child was Pansy.

I forgot Mary and Penny and stared in delight. My little sister had grown. She was as big as I had been when she was birthed. She was tall and beautiful, and not the least bit blue. She skipped and jumped, as if it was real hard to keep still. Oh! She was just like me when I was small-child young.

My heart felt stuffed full of happiness. There *really was* a happy place and Great-gran was there, and Pansy, and Katya too.

'Where's Dad?' I asked, while Penny and Mary open-mouth gaped.

'On the other side, waiting to guide us back. He sends his best love to you all . . . especially he sends it to Mam.'

I had no chance to ask more.

'Katya! You're *mended*,' Penny shrieked. 'I have worried about you so!'

'Is that your Ostrich?' Mary asked. She had always been fascinated by my tales of my crotchety gran.

'I may be an ostrich,' hissed my lovely lippy great-gran, 'but I have succeeded in being a lot more stubborn than you! You have miles to go yet, girl, if you wish to become a *real* character like me.'

Mary giggled. 'I'd never dare try, Great-gran Ostrich. You and Freya between you are stubborn enough for the whole wide world.'

'I'll get my stick with a nail to you!'

'You're as wicked and wonderful as Freya told me. I'll never be scared of you.'

Great-gran spluttered, and her crinkle face was as chuckle-bright as her eyes. She was shaking with laughter, but somehow still managed to hang on to our precious past-time babies.

The bright light began to fade. Great-gran offered us one last glimpse of her crooked smile. 'We will be here, waiting for the moment you have travelled life's pathway. And then, and only then, will we come back to greet you.'

'Great-gran,' I whispered, as their bodies grew sunshine-transparent, 'will you still help me with my magic?'

'Of course, Chime Child. Haven't I helped you always?'

The three of them vanished, only Great-gran's bellow-boom voice could be heard. 'One last thing, Freya. I like your friends, especially that mouthy Mary. For gorgio girls they're not bad, not bad at all! Now finish your magic . . . and be happy.'

I ignored the sound of the Reverend Plumpton sneaking around his own church, and carefully picked up the glass containing the gold and silver water to sprinkle some over Penny.

'Yellow-yolk sun, white bright silver, safety shell of thrice-blessed holy water. I invoke your power. I wish Penny's tongue free for ever. I ask only that she should be happy.'

'Amen,' Mary and Penny said together.

Out of the corner of my eye I saw the vicar mime 'Amen'. I was pleased that even he had joined in. I knew he had seen no enchantment, just three little girls waiting for morning in a cold grey church. Our gods were very different, but their gift of healing was the same.

24 Resolution

With the magic of gold and silver water, Pudding Pot Penny vanished for ever. Her dark-despair eyes turned to hazel-brown sparkles, her face dimple-crinkled with the joy of knowing that Katya was happy.

'I'm glad I made friends with my mother,' Penny told us. 'The doctors say she can come home soon. This time things will be *so* different.'

'Why?'

Penny smiled, and her face lit starshine bright. 'Maybe Katya was needed . . . to be Pansy's friend. Anyway, I was wrong to blame Norman.'

'Of course, Uncle Norman is Katya's father,' Mary exclaimed, her curiousness burst like an over-stretched bubble.

Penny nodded.

I felt frilly-frock foolish as the jigsaw pieces slotted into place. Penny had made life snake-pit difficult, blaming her mum for rushing to meet Uncle

Norman, and him for just being. *He* had even reminded me that love and hate were clingy close, yet *still* I'd failed to see. *She'd been too scratch-heart scared to love him.*

'Uncle Norman won't dump you. You won't be abandoned *twice*.'

'No,' Mary said firmly. 'He's far too kind.'

'Yes,' Penny told us. 'I know that now.'

I felt full-heart happy. The magic was done. I was free to go home at last.

25 The Legacy

As soon as I touched home earth I realised why Great-gran had been holding the baby Katya and my sister Pansy, in church. A circle of cold grey earth replaced the spot where her wagon had stood.

'You never told me that she died!' I accused, letting go of Tashar's hand, and running to my mam showing tickle-pearl tears.

'You *know*. You just haven't *accepted*,' Mam told me calmly. 'You saw her.'

She was right. Salty streaks dried on my face. 'And she really heard Penny's chitter-chatter tongue?'

'She heard! Great-gran never misses anything. Our old Ostrich can't change her ways so soon.'

I had to laugh. My mam was right, it was difficult to imagine Great-gran missing out on a bit of nosiness.

'The place seems so quiet without her.'

'It won't be now *you're* back,' my mam told me. 'Now come, we have something to show you.'

The whole family led me to the other side of the great old hedge. My eyes grew wide-eyed shocked. There before me were the horses *and* Great-gran's happy vardo. There was no sign of burn at all!

I raced up to the beautiful vardo and stroked the ancient wooden wheels. My hands tingled in its power.

'Why? Why, after all that she said, is it not dust-ash burned?'

'I built her a box,' Tashar explained proudly. 'I built it just like the vardo . . . exactly to match. She said it would do.'

'Which meant it was *perfect*,' Mam said proudly. 'So the proper vardo is yours, a reminder that Great-gran is *still* here to help you with your magic.'

A Little Gypsy History

Gypsies are a nomadic people. Their origins have become a little lost in the mists of time.

It is almost certain that the gypsy originated in India. They were most likely to have been a tent dwelling people of fairly low caste.

The word gypsy is actually a corruption of the word Egyptian, and one theory was that the gypsy may have originated in Little Egypt, which in itself is confusing, as this has been variously considered to be Egypt, Little Armenia and Epirus.

Gypsies are known as Arzigans or Athinganoi in Asia Minor. These names are derived from an Indian sub caste, with the meaning, 'Not to be touched'. Many of them were said to earn their living by sorcery.

Romanes is predominately a spoken language, passed from mouth to mouth, in a travelling culture.

The backbone of the Romany language is Indian, corrupted, or adapted, over the passage of time, with additions from countries such as Iran (Persia), Romania, Turkey, Hungary and, eventually, Western Europe.

For a people, so widely travelled, it is surprising how constant the Romanes language is, despite regional variations. This is probably due more to dialect than evolution. The pure Romany gypsies, that I have spoken to are extremely proud of still having a language that can be understood, no matter where they travel.

True Romanies remain a proud race, with a very individual culture, which, even if not strictly adhered to today, is of great historic importance. Their greatest fear seems to be the intrusion into their lifestyle caused by the modern Traveller.

Romany gypsies have always considered themselves to be a race apart. I believe that they should be allowed to remain so. It would be a great loss to society if a culture that has existed so successfully, for so long, should be destroyed.

Romany Words Used

Athinganoi	a particular tribal caste
Bori Bori	big friend
Bubbo	baby
Buni Manridi	honey cake
Chavi(s)	girl(s)
Chavo	boy
Chiriko	bird
Choviar	witch
Didakai	half-Romany
Drúkkerébema	prophesy
Gorgio	non-gypsy
Hotchi-witchi	hedgehog
Juvel	Romany women
Kackaratchi	magpie
Kokko	uncle
Koshti Bok	good luck
Motto	drunk

Mul-sko-dud	will-o'-the-wisp
Patteran	road sign
Poshrat	half-blood
Prala	brother
Rokker	talk
Romnichals	Romany men
Sastra Pot	stew
Shoshi	rabbit
Vardo	gypsy wagon